The Cupcake Diaries:
Recipe for Love

Sweet, Fun-loving
Romance!

Darlene Panzera

THE CUPCAKE DIARIES
Recipe for Love

DARLENE PANZERA

AVONIMPULSE
An Imprint of HarperCollinsPublishers

Excerpt from *The Cupcake Diaries: Sweet On You* copyright © 2013 by Darlene Panzera.

Excerpt from *The Cupcake Diaries: Taste of Romance* copyright © 2013 by Darlene Panzera.

Excerpt from *Stealing Home* copyright © 2013 by Candice Wakoff.

Excerpt from *Lucky Like Us* copyright © 2013 by Jennifer Ryan.

Excerpt from *Stuck On You* copyright © 2013 by Cheryl Harper.

Excerpt from *The Right Bride* copyright © 2013 by Jennifer Ryan.

Excerpt from *Lachlan's Bride* copyright © 2013 by Kathleen Harrington.

EPub Edition MAY 2013 ISBN: 9780062242686

Print Edition ISBN: 9780062242693

JV 10 9 8 7 6 5 4 3 2 1

For my children,
Samantha, Robert, and Jason

Chapter One

Life is uncertain. Eat dessert first.

—Ernestine Ulmer

RACHEL PUSHED THROUGH the double doors of the kitchen, took one look at the masked man at the counter, and dropped the freshly baked tray of cupcakes on the floor.

Did he plan to rob Creative Cupcakes, demand she hand over the money from the cash register? Her eyes darted around the frilly pink-and-white shop. The loud clang of the metal bakery pan hitting the tile had caused several customers sitting at the tables to glance in her direction. Would the masked man threaten the other people as well? How could she protect them?

She stepped over the white-frosted chocolate mess by

her feet, tried to judge the distance to the telephone on the wall, and turned her attention back to the masked man before her. Maybe he wasn't a robber but someone dressed for a costume party or play. The man with the black masquerade mask covering the upper half of his face also wore a black cape.

"If this is a holdup, you picked the wrong place, Zorro." She tossed her fiery red curls over her shoulder with false bravado and laid a protective hand across the old bell-ringing register. "We don't have any money."

His hazel eyes gleamed through the holes in the mask, and he flashed her a disarming smile. "Maybe I can help with that."

He turned his hand to show an empty palm, and relief flooded over her. No gun. Then he closed his fingers and swung his fist around in the air three times. When he opened his palm again, he held a quarter, which he tossed in her direction.

Rachel caught the coin and laughed. "You're a magician."

"Mike the Magnificent," he said, extending his cape wide with one arm and taking a bow. "I'm here for the Lockwell party."

Rachel pointed to the door leading to the back party room. The space had originally been a tattoo shop, but the tattoo artist relocated to the rental next door. "The Lockwells aren't here yet. The party doesn't start until three."

"I came early to set up before the kids arrive," Mike told her. "Can't have them discovering my secrets."

"No, I guess not," Rachel agreed. "If they did, Mike the magician might not be so magnificent."

"Magnificence is hard to maintain." His lips twitched, as if suppressing a grin. "Are you Andi?"

She shook her head. "Rachel, Creative Cupcakes' stupendous co-owner, baker, and promoter."

This time a grin did escape his mouth, which led her to notice his strong, masculine jawline.

"Tell me, Rachel, what is it that makes you so stupendous?"

She gave him her most flirtatious smile. "Sorry, I can't reveal my secrets either."

"Afraid if I found out the truth, I might not think you're so impressively great?"

Rachel froze, fearing Mike the magician might be a mind reader as well. Careful to keep her smile intact, she forced herself to laugh off his comment.

"I just don't think it's nice to brag," she responded playfully.

"Chicken," he taunted in an equally playful tone as he made his way toward the party room door.

Despite the uneasy feeling he'd discovered more about her in three minutes than most men did in three years, she wished he'd stayed to chat a few minutes more.

Andi Burke, wearing one of the new, hot-pink Creative Cupcakes bibbed aprons, came in from the kitchen and stared at the cupcake mess on the floor. "What happened here?"

"Zorro came in, gave me a panic attack, and the tray slipped out of my hands." Rachel grabbed a couple of paper towels and squatted down to scoop up the crumpled cake and splattered frosting before her OCD kitchen safety friend could comment further. "Don't worry, I'll take care of the mess."

"I should have told you Officer Lockwell hired a magician for his daughter's birthday party." Andi bent to help her, and when they stood back up, she asked, "Did you speak to Mike?"

Rachel nodded, her gaze on the connecting door to the party room as it opened, and Mike reappeared. Tipping his head toward them as he walked across the floor, he said, "Good afternoon, ladies."

Mike went out the front door, and Rachel hurried around the display case of cupcakes and crossed over to the shop's square, six-foot-high, street-side window. She leaned her head toward the glass and watched him take four three-by-three-foot black painted boxes out of the back of a van.

"You should go after him," Andi teased, her voice filled with amusement. "He's very handsome."

"How can you tell?" Rachel drew away from the window, afraid Mike might catch her spying on him. "He's got a black mask covering the upper half of his face. He could have sunken eyes, shaved eyebrows, and facial tattoos."

Andi laughed. "He doesn't, and I know you like guys with dark hair. He's not as tall as my Jake, but he's still got a great build."

"Better not let Jake hear you say that," Rachel retorted. "And how do you know he has a great build? The guy's wrapped in a cape."

"I've seen him before," Andi said. "Without the cape."

"Where?"

"His photo was in the newspaper two weeks ago," Andi confided. "The senior editor at the *Astoria Sun* assigned Jake to write an article on Mike Palmer's set models."

"What are you talking about?"

"Mike Palmer created the miniature model replica of the medieval city of Hilltop for the movie *Battle for Warrior Mountain* and worked on set pieces for many other movies filmed around Astoria. His structural designs are so intricate that when the camera zooms in close, it looks real."

Mike returned through the front door, wheeling in the black boxes on an orange dolly. Rachel caught her breath as he looked her way before proceeding toward the party room with his equipment. Did the masked man find her as intriguing as she found him?

Andi's younger sister, Kim, came in from the kitchen with a large tray of red velvet cupcakes with cherry cream cheese frosting. The three of them together, with Andi's boyfriend, Jake Hartman, as their financial partner, had managed to open Creative Cupcakes a month and a half earlier.

"Who's he?" Kim asked. She placed the cupcakes on the marble counter and pointed toward the billowing black cape of the magician.

"Mike the Magnificent," Rachel said dreamily.

OFFICER IAN LOCKWELL, his wife, son, and daughter entered the shop a short while later. The first time Rachel had met him, he'd written her a parking ticket. Since then, he had helped chase off a group of fanatical Zumba dancers who were trying to shut down Creative Cupcakes and had become one of their biggest supporters. Both were good reasons for her to reverse her original harsh feelings toward the blond, burly man.

"Happy Birthday, Caitlin," Rachel greeted his six-year-old daughter. "Ready for the magic show?"

"I hope he pulls a rabbit out of his hat," Caitlin said, her eyes sparkling. "I asked for a rabbit for my birthday."

"She wanted one last month for Easter," Officer Lockwell confided. "But I told her the bunnies were busy delivering eggs."

"There are always more rabbits in April," Andi told Caitlin and winked conspiratorially at her father. "Aren't there?"

Officer Lockwell shifted his gaze to the ceiling.

"Should we go to the party room?" Rachel asked, leading the way.

"Here are two more," Jake Hartman said, ushering his little girl, Taylor, and Andi's daughter, Mia, into the shop. Both six-year-olds attended the same kindergarten class as Caitlin at Astor Elementary.

Andi stepped forward and gave Jake a kiss before he had to head back to work at the newspaper office.

"Is he a real magician, Mom?" Mia asked Andi, hugging her legs as Mike the Magnificent came out to welcome them.

"As real as they get," Andi assured her.

Rachel exchanged a look with Andi above Mia's head and smiled. "I wonder if he needs an assistant."

IN THE PRIVACY of the kitchen, Andi pulled the pink bandana off Rachel's hair. "That's better. Now primp your curls."

"And don't forget to swing your hips as you serve the cupcakes," Kim added. "Maybe Magic Mike will wave his wand and whisk you under his cape for a kiss."

"I can hope," Rachel said. "I haven't had a date in two weeks."

"Is that a new record?" Andi teased.

"Almost."

"Maybe if you kept one guy around long enough, you wouldn't have to worry about finding a date," Kim said, arching one of her delicate dark eyebrows.

"Oh, no!" Rachel shook her head. "Rule number one: *Never* date the same man three times in a row. First dates are fabulous, second dates fun, but third dates? That's when guys start to think they freaking know you, and the relationship fails. Better to stick with two dates and forget the rest."

"Jake and I continue to have fun," Andi argued.

"That's because you and Jake are made for each other." Rachel picked up the tray of cupcakes they'd decorated to look like white rabbits peeking out from chocolate top hats. "And so far, I haven't met any man who looks at me the way he looks at you. If I *did*," she said, pausing to make sure her friend got the hint, "I'd marry him."

Andi pushed a strand of her long, dark blond hair behind her ear and blushed. "Maybe Mike will be your man."

"Maybe," Rachel conceded and smiled. "But every relationship starts with a first date."

WHEN RACHEL ENTERED the room, Mike was in the middle of performing a card trick. She scanned the faces of the two dozen kids sitting at the long, rectangular tables covered with pink partyware and colorful birthday presents. Mike did a good job of holding their attention. They sat in wide-eyed fascination. Not one of them noticed her as she distributed the cupcakes to each place setting.

Next, Mike the Magnificent showed the audience the inside of his empty black top hat. Placing the hat right-side up on one of his black boxes, he waved his wand over the top and quickly flipped the hat upside down again. Rachel smiled as he invited the birthday girl up to the hat. The six-year-old reached her hand in and pulled out a fake toy bunny with big, white floppy ears.

Caitlin looked at Mike, her eyes betraying her disappointment, then mumbled, "Thanks."

"Were you hoping for a real rabbit?" Mike asked her.

Caitlin nodded.

"Let's try that again." Mike told Caitlin to put the stuffed bunny back into the hat. Then he turned the hat over and placed it down on the black box again. He waved the wand. This time when he turned the hat over a live rabbit with big, white floppy ears poked its head up over the top of the rim.

Caitlin let out an excited squeal, and Rachel laughed. Mike the Magnificent was good with the kids and a good magician. How did he do it? She stared at the box and the black hat and couldn't tell how he'd been able to make the switch. Dodging a couple of the strings that hung down from the balloons bobbing against the ceiling, she moved closer.

"Just the person I was looking for," Mike said, catching her eye. "Rachel, could you come up here for a moment?"

"Certainly." Rachel gave him a wide smile and moved to his side. "What would you like me to do?"

"Get in the box."

Rachel glanced at the large horizontal black box resting upon two sawhorses in the middle of the room. It looked eerily like a coffin.

"And take off your shoes," he added under his breath.

Rachel stepped out of her pink pumps, and when Mike moved aside the black curtain covering the box, she slid inside.

"How about a pillow?" Mike asked.

"A pillow would be nice," she said.

His large, warm hand cupped the back of her head as he placed the white cushion beneath her, and his gaze locked with hers. "Are you married?"

Rachel's eyes widened. "No."

"Have a steady boyfriend?"

Rachel shook her head.

"Good," Mike said and grinned at the audience. "I

won't have to worry about anyone coming after me if something goes wrong."

"What do you mean, '*if something goes wrong*'?" she demanded.

He held up a carpenter's saw with a very large, jagged blade, and the kids in the audience giggled with delight.

"He's going to saw her in half!" Mia exclaimed. "I don't think my mommy will like that. How will Rachel help my mom bake cupcakes?"

"Saw me in half?" Rachel gasped and stared up at Mike. How did this trick work? He wasn't really going to come near her with that saw, was he? "I . . . uh . . . have a slight fear of blades. If I get hurt, do you have a girlfriend or wife I can complain to?"

Mike grinned. "No wife. But if you survive, maybe I'll marry you."

The young audience edged forward in anticipation, probably wondering if they'd see blood or hear her scream.

Rachel had done some pretty crazy things in the past to get a date, but this ridiculous stunt had to top them all. "I really am afraid of blades," she said, her voice raised to a high-pitched squeak.

"Don't worry; I've only killed two people in the past," Mike reassured her, then leaned down to whisper in her ear, "Roll to your side and curl up in a ball."

Rachel did as she was told and faced the audience. There was more room in the box than she'd first supposed. Mike made a few quick adjustments, and an inside board slid up against her feet. Then he raised the shark-toothed blade above her and began to saw the outside of the box in two. The box rattled, and the fresh sawdust made her sneeze, making the kids laugh.

"Does it hurt?" Caitlin asked.

"Not yet," Rachel admitted.

"Here we go," Mike announced.

Rachel closed her eyes, and memories of her uncle filled her mind. Distracted, he'd slipped while working a circular saw and cut off three of his fingers. Blood spurt in every direction. She'd been seven and stood by his side when it happened.

Everyone in the room shouted as Mike pulled the black boxes apart. Rachel frowned. She didn't feel any different.

"Rachel, are you alive?" Mia called out.

"Yes, I'm still here."

Jake's daughter, Taylor, pointed. "Her feet are sticking out of the other half of the box."

"How do you know those feet are mine?" Rachel challenged, knowing her bare toes were curled beneath her.

Caitlin laughed. "They are wearing your pink shoes."

Rachel craned her head around to see the other half of the black box several feet away. The two flesh-colored, lifelike feet sticking out of the end wore her pink pumps.

"How 'bout we put Rachel back together?" Mike suggested.

The kids clapped and cheered.

Moving the two boxes back together, Mike motioned for her to slide out of the first wooden compartment. Then he removed the set of fake feet out of the second compartment and gave her back her pink pumps. When she'd slipped them on, he took her hand and led her in front of the audience.

"She's back together again!" Mia exclaimed.

"Take a bow," Mike told her. "You've earned it"

"I survived." Rachel tilted her head and gave him a questioning look to remind him of his earlier words. But he didn't ask her to marry him.

He didn't even ask her for a date.

Disappointed, Rachel left the party and headed back to the kitchen, where Andi and Kim waited for a progress report.

"Does he like you?" Andi asked.

"Oh, yes," Rachel said and swallowed the knot in the back of her throat. "He called me a 'good sport.'"

Chapter Two

It's not that chocolates are a substitute for love.
Love is a substitute for chocolate. Chocolate is,
let's face it, far more reliable than a man.

—Miranda Ingram

RACHEL PUT THE pink bandana back over her hair and tried not to think about Mike the Magnificent any longer. If he wasn't interested in her, then so be it. She didn't need him.

"Who knows?" Andi said, her voice filled with compassion. "The next guy through the door could be the man of your dreams. Maybe he'll be dressed as Superman."

Rachel managed a short laugh. "That's comforting."

"Or it could be the stooped, gray-haired building owner," Kim warned. "He said he'd be by this evening."

"Eat a chocolate cupcake, and you'll feel better," Andi instructed. "Then help tally receipts and count out money for rent."

Rachel nodded to the Cupcake Diary Andi held in her hands, the three-ring binder containing all their notes pertaining to the cupcake business. "How are we doing?"

"When Jake balanced the financial books, he said Creative Cupcakes is doing okay, but we need to do better," Andi informed her. "There's still no money for extras."

Kim set her paintbrush on the plate of food gels and turned in her seat at the front table where she'd been decorating the smooth fondant tops of a dozen vanilla truffle cupcakes. "Maybe we shouldn't have accepted the building owner's offer to use the extra space in the back for a party room."

Rachel frowned. "I love the party room."

"I have several groups interested in booking the space for different nights of the week," Andi said, tapping the list in the Cupcake Diary with her pencil. "And once the shop starts making more money, I'd love to go on vacation. Someplace warm—with Jake."

"After working so hard to open Creative Cupcakes, we could all use a vacation," Kim agreed. "But before I can afford to travel, I need to rent a gallery space in Portland to display my artwork."

Rachel thought of her sick grandfather who had drained her mother's bank account with medical bills. "We need more customers."

All three of them lifted their gaze to the golden cupcake cutter, the size of a short sword, which hung on the pink pin-striped wall above their heads. The shiny victory blade had been a symbol of success after their struggle to open the shop. Now it sat, unused, between Kim's unsold watercolor paintings as a stark reminder that starting a business was only part of the battle. Now they needed to *stay* in business.

Evening fog drifted in ghost-like wisps through the streets outside Creative Cupcakes' window. The inside of the shop resembled a ghost town, too. The tables and chairs in the dining area and the stools in front of the marble counter sat empty. The sweet, delicious multiflavored cupcakes in the glass display case remained untouched.

Andi straightened her shoulders and pointed toward the large storefront window. "Here comes a customer now."

The bells on the front door jingled as it opened, and in walked a tall blond man with an impressive build. Except for his black beret, he was dressed all in white from the collar of his dress shirt straight down to his leather wing tip shoes.

Kim nudged Rachel and whispered, "Maybe he's an angel sent to answer our prayers."

Rachel pursed her lips. "He looks more like Chef Ramsey on *Hell's Kitchen*."

"Can we help you?" Andi asked.

"I'll taste one of your bite-size tiramisu cakes," he said, his accent distinctively French.

"Great choice," Rachel told him. She opened the display case while Andi took his money, and the strong scent of the coffee-and-mascarpone whipped frosting wafted into the air. "Dusted with cocoa, these moist, creamy cupcakes are guaranteed to melt in your mouth and keep you coming back for more."

"I'll be the judge of that," the Frenchman replied. Lifting the miniature cupcake to his mouth, he took a bite, paused a few seconds to chew, then walked over to the nearest garbage can and spit it out. "How long have you been in business?"

Rachel glanced at the can and frowned. "Six weeks."

"From where did you gather your recipes?"

"Most of them were my mother's," Andi said, her voice filled with pride. "And some I've created on my own."

"And your credentials?"

Andi smiled. "My mother taught me to bake."

"Not one of you attended a school for culinary arts?"

Andi hesitated, then gave an almost imperceptible shake of her head. Kim remained stock-still and silent. Rachel narrowed her gaze and tried to decipher exactly what the guy was up to.

"I assumed as much," he said, sweeping his gaze around the room. "I am Gaston Pierre Hollande. Undoubtedly you have heard of me."

Rachel looked at Andi and Kim and shrugged.

"Gaston Pierre Hollande, crowned the Prince of Pastry and awarded the grand champion trophy on the reality TV show *Extreme Bake-off?*" he prompted.

"Sorry," Rachel said, "I must have missed that one."

"It appears that you missed them all if you consider this a bake shop." He sniffed and stepped forward to study the other cupcakes in the display case. "You only serve cupcakes? No other bakery items?"

"We are Creative *Cupcakes*," Andi emphasized, lifting her chin. "Cupcakes are our specialty."

"Not for long," he informed them brusquely. "I have come here tonight to evaluate my competition, but I can see this is no competition at all. If anyone needs help, it is you. For while my bakery, the prominent Hollande's French Pastry Parlor, draws crowds of customers through its doors with its wide menu of fine delicacies, your shop sits here empty."

"We are about to close for the night," Kim told him.

"You will soon close forever," Gaston boasted. "As will every other bakery in town." He eyed them with contempt. "I did not see your name on the list of vendors for Astoria's Crab, Seafood, and Wine Festival. Are you not going?"

Rachel shot another glance toward her friends and bit her lower lip. She didn't even think of promoting their cupcakes at the festival. They'd set up a booth at the Relay for Life fundraiser and held a grand opening party, and she'd used her computer skills to create a website, Facebook page, and Twitter account. But most of their energy was directed toward the day-to-day details of baking and selling at the shop.

"My bakery has a premier location within the festival building, and when the weekend is over, everyone in Astoria, Oregon, and the whole Northwest will know Hollande's French Pastry Parlor is number one."

"Yeah," Andi said, her sudden smile giving way to a smirk. "Good luck with that."

"My success is not a result of luck, but talent," he insisted.

"Maybe we'll sign up," Rachel said, standing on her tiptoes to look him straight in the eye.

"*Au contraire!* The vendor slots for the festival were sold out long ago," Gaston told them, his face smug. "You are too late."

Rachel shrugged, careful to keep her expression indifferent. "I doubt cupcakes belong at the Crab, Seafood, and Wine Festival anyway."

"Not as creative as your name suggests, no?" he taunted.

Mike came out of the back party room, and Gaston's forehead creased fourfold as he took in the magician's costume. Directing his attention back to the three women, he asked, "You're working with clowns?"

Rachel scowled. "He's not a clown; he's a magician."

"I meant clown as in 'buffoon,'" he retorted, jutting out his cleft chin.

Mike drew close to Rachel's side. "Who's this?"

"The Prince of Pastry."

Gaston handed Mike a business card from his back pocket. "If you need to recommend a real bakery, here is my number."

Mike waved his hands, and the business card shot into the air and circled round and round his body until it finally swung inside the plastic-lined barrel beside him.

"You fool! What are you doing?" Gaston demanded, his hat falling off in his aggravated attempt to reclaim the card.

Andi's daughter, Mia, ran from the doorway of the party room to the barrel and peered in. "He made it float into the garbage can!"

Andi nodded. "Where it should be."

Mike stooped down to pick up Gaston's hat from the floor.

"Have you no respect?" Gaston barked, his fair face turning red as he narrowed his beady gaze on the magician. "Give me back my beret!"

Mike complied, and Gaston slapped his hat back on his head. A moment later, his eyes widened, and taking the hat off again, he looked inside.

Mia gasped, her mouth transformed into a perfect O.

Rachel sneaked a quick glance at Mike and let out a laugh. Andi, Kim, and many of the others coming from the party room laughed, too. The only one not laughing was Gaston—maybe because his head was covered in the remains of a smashed chocolate cupcake with coconut cream filling

"Who's the buffoon now?" Mike challenged.

Gaston Pierre Hollande let out a high-pitched, explosive word, which Rachel assumed to be a French curse, and stomped his foot. "Make no mistake," Gaston declared, his tone ten times haughtier than when he'd first walked in, "Hollande's French Pastry Parlor will be number one."

The door slammed behind him on his way out, and Andi gestured to the Frenchman as he passed outside the front window. "How did a cupcake get into his hat?"

"Mike swiped it off the counter with his hand behind his back," Rachel said, smiling.

"Discovering my secrets?" Mike asked, giving her an amused look. He took out his wallet. "How much do I owe you?"

"You don't owe us anything," Rachel told him. "You did us a favor. That man has an ego larger than the Astoria–Megler Bridge."

"I overheard the way he talked to you, and I didn't like it," Mike said, and a muscle jumped along the side of his jaw. "My sister dated someone with a similar attitude. It didn't end well."

"What happened?"

"He broke her heart."

A string of faces floated through Rachel's mind. The ones who had managed to get too close were the ones who had broken *her* heart. "Has she met anyone else since?"

"No."

Rachel recalled the boys in grade school who teased her for her freckles and red hair. A few years later, after she'd used a myriad of beauty products to change her appearance, her high school boyfriend dumped her for someone more popular because she didn't party enough. Then when she went to college and passed herself off as "the party girl," her college sweetheart took her for granted. That's when she'd initiated the two-date limit to keep her relationships fresh and exciting and her heart intact. So far, it had worked.

"Rachel?"

She snapped out of her revelry, glanced toward the front door, where Andi and Kim stood waving goodbye to the party guests, and refocused on the masked magician in front of her. "Did you say something?"

"I asked for your phone number, but you look like you've seen a ghost."

Funny how memories can haunt you, she thought. She cocked her head, relishing the thought of a temporary diversion. "You want my phone number?"

"Of course," he said, and his mouth twitched into a subtle grin. "Unless you don't want to give it to me."

"Depends," Rachel teased. "Will you call to ask me to be the one you saw in half at your next magic show, or will you use it to ask me out?"

"I'm asking you out now. I only need your phone number to confirm the details."

Rachel gave him a big smile, turned toward her friends, and called out, "Andi, Kim, where's a pen?"

TEN O'CLOCK MONDAY morning, Rachel sprawled across her quilted patchwork bed, her cell phone to her ear, and waited for the coordinator of the Crab, Seafood, and Wine Festival to answer.

"The deadline for sign-ups was three months ago," the woman told her.

Rachel's spirits sank, but then there was another voice in the background speaking to the woman in charge.

"You may be in luck," the woman continued. "It seems one of our other food vendors has an emergency and needs to pull out. I can let you have his space."

"Great. How much?"

"A ten-by-ten aisle space rents for four hundred dollars."

Rachel thought of Creative Cupcakes' limited bank account and then Gaston's smug face. The event brought thousands of people into town each year, many from neighboring states, and with them came a boatload of money. She hadn't associated cupcakes with crab, seafood, and wine, but, hey, why not? Cupcakes tasted good no matter where you ate them, didn't they?

A large percentage of the locals took on double-, sometimes triple-duty temporary jobs during the weekend festival to both help out and earn extra cash. Last year her postman drove one of the school buses transporting people back and forth from the various hotels in town to the fairgrounds. Andi had once worked as a hired hand serving crab in the main dining hall. And she herself had once stood near the entrance stamping hands and collecting the fairgoers' festival fee.

Still, $400 was a lot of money.

"Can I discuss this with my business partners and get back to you on this?" Rachel asked.

"Only if you can get back to me within the next ten minutes," the woman replied. "I know others who would be interested in taking the space."

Rachel called Andi at home. No answer. Next, she called Kim at the cupcake shop and didn't get a hold of her either. She called Jake at his day job working at the office of the *Astoria Sun*, but he was out on assignment. And not one of them answered when she called their cell phones.

What should she do? She hated making a decision without consulting her friends, but this was an opportunity too big to miss. Hoping she wouldn't regret her choice, she called back the woman in charge of the Astoria Crab, Seafood, and Wine Festival.

"Yes," Rachel said, her voice resolute. "We'll take it."

If they didn't make any money at the festival, Rachel would take responsibility and suffer the loss from her own earnings from the cupcake shop. She might not be able to afford gas for her car, but Kim didn't have a vehicle and managed to get around. She could do the same.

She flipped open the latest issue of *Beauty, Fashion, and Glamour* magazine to an article titled, "Top Ten Tips: How to Make Men Fall Irresistibly in Love with You."

Her cell phone buzzed, and she wondered which of her business partners had finally received her message. Instead, it was a text from the magician, Mike Palmer.

Are you available for dinner tonight?

They had agreed on dinner at the new seafood restaurant on pier 39 in the renovated Bumble Bee Hanthorn Cannery but hadn't decided what night would suit both of their schedules.

Smiling, she rolled over on the bed and punched in her reply. *Need to work. How bout this weekend? Oops. Scratch that. Our shop @ the Crab & Wine fest.*

Mike responded a few seconds later. *Next Wednesday?*

She tried to imagine what he might look like without the mysterious black mask. Would he live up to her expectations? After checking her calendar, she sent back: *It's a date.*

The deep rumble of her mother's car sounded in the driveway, and Rachel pushed aside the flimsy lace curtain to look out her second-story garage apartment window. Tossing her cell phone on the dresser filled with perfume, nail polish, and makeup, she hurried down the steps.

"You're home early," Rachel said, as her mom got out of the beat-up minivan.

"I had to take your grandfather to his doctor's appointment."

"How did it go?"

"As well as it could."

Her mother's face appeared more haggard than usual. Could be from the two jobs she took on to pay her grandfather's medical bills.

"Rachel, help me get your grandfather into the house, please."

She obeyed and opened the passenger side of the car. Grandpa Lewy had his wispy white head tilted back, and he was snoring with his mouth wide open. Her mother gave him a gentle shake, and the old man woke with a start.

"I told you I like my eggs hard-boiled," he scolded.

Rachel and her mother pulled him out of the seat, and balancing his weight between them, they managed to lead him into the house.

"When were you hired? You aren't the regular nurse who comes in," Rachel's grandpa said, looking up into her face. "Do I know you?"

"Yes," Rachel answered, meeting her mother's gaze as they helped him into his rocker. "I'm your granddaughter."

"I'm related to you?" The old man laughed. "Your hair is as red as a twelve-pound radish!"

"So was yours back in the day," Rachel's mom chided.

A few minutes later, Grandpa Lewy was comfortably snoring once again.

"Would you like breakfast?" Rachel followed her mother down the hall. "Or should I get out the leftover chicken-and-rice casserole from last night?"

"I'm not hungry."

"How about I fix you some tea and maybe we could talk?" Rachel asked hopefully.

"I have to sleep now so I can work tonight." Her mother patted her hand and shot her a look of compassion. "Soon?"

Rachel had heard her mother say "soon" for the last decade. "I thought life would be easier with the state-certified nurse coming to watch over him every day."

"His Alzheimer's is getting worse," her mother confided. "The doctor told me there's a new treatment that could help, but it's deemed 'experimental,' and the insurance won't cover it. I might have to find extra work."

"Mom, no!" Rachel protested. "You're already working two jobs. I can't remember the last time we spent a whole day together. If you take on more hours, I'll never see you."

"What choice do I have?"

"Let me help," Rachel told her. "Creative Cupcakes still needs to grow, but I'll give you whatever I can each week."

"We need $10,000," her mom said wearily, "and if he doesn't start the treatment soon, we could lose him."

"Lose Grandpa?" Rachel swallowed hard. It seemed like they'd just lost her father not too long ago. Drowned in a boating accident. She couldn't lose Grandpa Lewy, too. Out of all her family, he was the one she'd always related to best.

She remembered her grandfather running around the beach, his bright red hair waving in the wind as he chased her through the tide pools when she was a little girl. In a family of redheads, tempers tended to flare, like hers did when they moved from Long Beach, Washington, to Astoria when she was in the first grade.

The kids in her new class at school took one look at her ruddy freckles and flaming hair and called her "the Sunkist Monster" because she was all orange. She'd exploded into a rage and promised revenge, but her fuse was doused by the tears that followed. It was her grandfather who had pulled her close, cradled her in his arms, and told her not to listen to them.

"There will be at least one other girl eager to be your friend, if you look hard enough," he predicted.

He was right. Next door to their new house there were two girls, a blonde about her age and the dark-haired sister who was four years younger. Through the years they'd fought and played, but they always stuck together when it mattered most. Who knew they'd end up opening a cupcake shop together?

Harnessing her Irish temper into firm resolve, she pushed her voice past the ache in her throat. "Mom?"

Her mother had walked down the hall, but upon hearing her name, she paused and looked back.

"I'll help you get the money for Grandpa's treatment."

Her mother nodded, gave her a brief smile that didn't offer much hope, and disappeared into her bedroom.

Rachel didn't know how she'd get the money, but she and her two best friends didn't know how to open a cupcake shop either when the crazy idea first sprouted in their heads.

Miracles could happen. All she needed to do was believe.

Chapter Three

Put "eat chocolate" at the top of your list of things to do today. That way, at least you'll get one thing done.

—Author unknown

"I KNOW THREE days doesn't give us much time to prepare," Rachel said, casting a glance at Andi and Kim as they boxed up several dozen chocolate cupcakes. "But I believe setting up a booth at the Crab, Seafood, and Wine Festival is a good investment. If it weren't, Gaston Pierre Hollande would never have signed up. Besides, who doesn't love a good party?"

"Wish I had your faith." Kim shook her head. "How are we going to bake enough cupcakes for both the shop and the festival before this weekend?"

"We can do it," Andi said, her face lit with excitement. "We'll have to bake like crazy and freeze some ahead of time, but Rachel's right. The profits could be amazing."

Kim gave them each a wary look. "Or not."

Leaving Andi's teenage babysitter, Heather, in charge of the shop, they walked down the street, crossed the railroad tracks, and carried the cardboard trays of cupcakes along the black paved path beneath the bridge.

"Coffee and cupcakes," Rachel called to the five people waiting for the Astoria Riverfront Trolley.

One man raised his hand. "I'll take one of each."

Rachel smiled as she served the order. "Here's a coupon for a dollar off your next Creative Cupcakes purchase. We're located straight up the block on Marine Drive."

A woman rushed toward Kim, her eyes wide. "Are those triple-chocolate caramel fudge?"

"Yes," Kim replied, "with double dark chocolate whipped buttercream icing—"

"And a cherry on top," the woman finished and drew in a deep breath. "I knew I smelled chocolate. How dare you scent the air with those fat-inducing treats!" She glanced in each direction up and down the Columbia River walkway, then pulled two twenty-dollar bills out of her purse. "Better give me the whole box so others don't fall prey to your temptations."

As the woman hurried away, Kim held up her empty hands. "Now *this* was a great idea. We should sell cupcakes along the waterfront every morning."

Andi agreed. "Hopefully, the people like the cupcakes so much they'll use the coupons to come into the shop."

"If we're going to compete against that French baker, we're going to need to step up our promo," Rachel said, serving two more tourists cups of coffee to go along with their cupcakes. "Why don't we start serving fresh brewed coffee and specialty tea in the shop to help wash down the cupcakes?"

"Don't forget the kids," Andi said as they moved farther along the waterfront walk. "Mia and Taylor will want milk or juice."

"Milkshakes," Kim added. "Chocolate, vanilla, and strawberry milkshakes. All we would need is a few more ingredients and a couple blenders."

"I've read that some cupcake shops have started serving ice cream, but we'd need more freezer space." Andi hesitated. "We'll have to talk to Jake about that."

"Done," Rachel told her. "Look behind you."

Andi spun around and spotted the man behind her. "Jake! What are you doing here?"

Jake Hartman, wearing a white dress shirt and brown khakis matching the color of his hair, gave them all a welcoming grin.

"What if I told you I had a lead on a story about three obnoxious women wearing pink head scarves and pink bakery aprons who are terrorizing the waterfront with cupcakes?"

"What if I told you," Andi challenged, "the chief editor of the *Astoria Sun* said if we see a deranged madman reporter draw near our cupcakes to send him straight back to the office?"

Jake laughed, wrapped his arms around Andi's waist, and gave her a kiss. "I'm on lunch break."

Envy stabbed Rachel's heart, and she glanced at Kim. Andi's dark-haired younger sister returned the look as if to say, "Yeah, I know."

Kim hadn't dated since her steady boyfriend in college took off to Europe without her. She said she was concentrating on her career as an aspiring artist, but instead of painting canvases, most days she was painting the tops of cupcakes.

Not exactly the happily-ever-after Kim had been hoping for. Or Rachel either. While the two-date-only method was great at protecting a broken heart, it didn't do much mending.

Sometimes, although she'd never admit it, she wished she could find the kind of love Andi seemed to have found. The kind that lasts forever.

BACK AT THE shop, Andi placed sticker labels on the Tupperware bins and wrote the names of the ingredients in each one with a blue marker. "This is so we don't mix up the flour with the sugar."

"We sure don't want that to happen," Rachel said, a trickle of heat sliding into her cheeks. She'd put cornstarch instead of baking soda in the batter of cherry cupcakes earlier that morning. She thought her slip had gone unnoticed, but Andi caught her dumping the mix in the trash.

Rachel took a new three-ring binder filled with notebook paper out of a shopping bag and placed it on the counter. The cover sparkled with enough glittery images to grace Hollywood.

"What's that?" Andi asked, catching a glimpse over her shoulder.

"Our new Cupcake Diary. The other one was filled up."

"It's so glitzy I'll be afraid of getting it dirty," Kim said, coming around the counter to take a look.

Rachel tossed her red curls over her shoulder and opened the new binder to the first page. "We need to be more glitzy to outshine the competition."

Andi nodded. "You mean improve our public image with advertising?"

"But not *false* advertising," Kim warned. "We need to stay true to ourselves."

Rachel laughed. "What does that even mean?"

"It means," Kim said, giving her a direct look, "don't get carried away."

Rachel frowned. "Creative Cupcakes must have an effective promotion plan to fight back against our new French rival and stay in business."

"In addition to birthday parties, we now have three groups using the party room each week," Andi informed them. "Our children's cupcake camp program is on Tuesdays."

"Mia's kindergarten friends waste more cupcakes than they make," Rachel complained. "They need constant supervision, and they get flour and sugar everywhere."

"No wonder their parents are willing to pay to have them come," Kim added. "Some of them are monsters."

"The kids have fun learning to bake," Andi said, lifting her chin. "And the cupcake camp brings in good money. Almost as much as the Romance Writers who come on Thursdays."

"The Romance Writers are loyal customers," Rachel agreed. "Those women absolutely devour anything chocolate."

"I don't trust them," Kim said, shaking her head. "They're always leaning in as if listening to what we have to say and writing in their little notepads. I'm afraid they might be writing about us, and we'll end up in one of their books."

"A story about three women who run a cupcake shop in a small town and find romance?" Rachel smirked. "Doubt it."

Taking out a pen, she wrote in the new Cupcake Diary:

Kids camp (messy monsters): Tuesdays
Romance Writers (Chocoholics): Thursdays

"Who's the third group we have coming in?" Kim asked.

"The Saturday Night Cupcake Club," Andi replied. "More like a Lonely Hearts Club, if you ask me. Whoever in their group doesn't have a date on Saturday night can come commiserate and eat cupcakes together."

"Sounds pitiful," Rachel said. "You wouldn't catch me at one of their meetings."

"Me either," Kim agreed.

"They aren't any different from us," Andi said, crossing her arms over her chest. "Isn't that how Creative Cupcakes started? With the three of us commiserating over the fact we had no jobs, no money, and no men? Sometimes it's good to open up and talk about your feelings. The year after my divorce, I was alone. If I'd known about such a group, I might have gone, but I had *you*."

Rachel thought about their birthday tradition. Their birthdays were exactly four months apart, so they split a cupcake three ways and made goals for themselves from one birthday to the next, much easier than setting goals for a whole year. Their last goal was to open a cupcake shop.

Back at the beginning of March, on the night of Kim's twenty-sixth birthday, Andi had convinced a guy sitting at a table in the Captain's Port to give them his cupcake. That's how Jake and Andi had met, with Jake agreeing to split the cupcake in fourths and sharing with them. Shortly later he became their financial partner for the cupcake shop, and Andi's Mr. Romance.

Rachel nodded toward the Cupcake Diary. "Okay, so we have three groups for the party room, but what else can we do for promotion?"

"We could hand out a red carpet invitation to everyone at the Crab, Seafood, and Wine Festival to visit our shop and sample Creative Cupcakes' award-winning flavors," Andi teased.

"That's good!" Rachel turned back to the Cupcake Diary and wrote in bold block letters:

Red carpet invites.

A chuckle greeted them from the doorway, and Guy Armstrong, the middle-aged tattoo artist from the next building, walked toward them and leaned over the marble counter. "Maybe offer a buy-one-get-one-free deal. Like 'get a tattoo, get a cupcake.' Or 'order two dozen cupcakes and get five dollars off your next tattoo.'"

Kim waved a hand toward her watercolor paintings adorning the shop's interior walls. "Buy a painting, get a free cupcake?"

Rachel shook her head. "We need to—"

"Think smarter?" Andi suggested.

"Be more creative?" Kim offered.

"Play dirtier," Guy said, bobbing his white pony-tailed head and pushing the sleeves of his black shirt up his tattooed forearms. "I love it when you women cook up a scheme. Sometimes I miss having my shop in the back room, but you inspired me to go after my dream and expand the business. And now I have more customers than ever before."

"That's it," Rachel said, pointing her pen at him. "We need to expand. We need to offer catering services for weddings and . . . and . . . get a cupcake truck!"

Andi's and Kim's mouths popped open.

"The Cupcake Mobile," Guy mused. "Has a nice ring to it."

"Where would we find a delivery truck?" Rachel asked.

Guy grinned wide enough to reveal his missing tooth. "I think I could help you with that."

RACHEL WIPED CRUMBS off the table by the front window and heard an awful *click-clackity* commotion outside.

Lifting her gaze, she watched in horror as an old blue-and-yellow bread-loaf-shaped truck pulled up to the front curb. It almost looked like a trolley car except there were also three silver trumpet-shaped horns attached to the roof. This couldn't be the truck Guy had been referring to, could it? She spotted Jake and the tattoo artist sitting in the front seat. Andi arrived a minute later and parked Jake's blue convertible behind them.

"They're here," Rachel called to Kim.

Kim followed her out the door and stood by her side on the sidewalk. "Looks like an antique."

"I'm surprised it runs," Andi said, getting out of the car to join them. "Guy says it's been sitting in his garage for decades."

"More like a century," Kim said, her expression doubtful. "What year is it?"

"Nineteen thirty-three."

Rachel pursed her lips. "Eye-catching."

"Don't frown like that," Guy said, climbing out of the passenger side of the vehicle. "It's a fully-restored Helm's bakery truck, and Kim can paint colorful cupcakes all over it."

"I could," Kim agreed, and her face brightened.

"She can also paint the name, Creative Cupcakes, in big swirly letters across the back and sides with our phone number to advertise the shop," Andi suggested.

"With a motto," Rachel said, walking closer to the vehicle to look inside. "Creative Cupcakes should have a motto."

Kim laughed. "'No time to bake? Call Creative Cupcakes!'"

"'Sweet cakes for every occasion'?" Andi asked.

"'One bite and you'll know it's right' or 'Tasty treats for toothless tattoo artists,'" Guy joked. "Like me."

Rachel gave him a friendly poke in the shoulder. "'If you like to flirt, try our hip little dessert.'"

"Gaston Pierre Hollande would paint a picture of a sword like the one in the movie *Highlander* and use the main character's quote, 'There can be only one!'" Kim said with a grin.

"We have a sword," Andi reminded them. "Our golden cupcake cutter. Maybe we can stick it in a giant cupcake and put it on display like King Arthur's sword in the stone legend."

"I have a better idea," Rachel said and pointed to the side of the Cupcake Mobile as if she could already see the image. "We can be like the three musketeers and borrow their motto: 'All for one, one for all.' And over that a logo, with three cupcake cutters like crossed swords sticking into a cupcake, dividing it three ways."

"What about Jake?" Andi asked. "He's part of Creative Cupcakes, too."

Rachel nodded. "He can be the fourth musketeer in Alexandre Dumas' story, who joined them later."

"Just like our birthday tradition!" Andi exclaimed.

Kim nodded her approval, a big smile on her face. "Just like *us*."

ON FRIDAY, RACHEL and Andi loaded the Cupcake Mobile, left Kim in charge of the shop, and headed toward the Clatsop County Fairgrounds for the Crab, Seafood, and Wine Festival. Andi drove the truck, and Rachel followed behind in her own car since they would be leaving at different times.

They'd borrowed some folding tables from Guy for their booth in the main food tent and brought hundreds of cupcakes packed in stackable plastic containers. Andi had also found pink tablecloths to match their pink bandanas and aprons.

Upon arrival they were given their ten-by-ten space between a wine vendor and another food vendor selling crab and melted cheese on thick, crusty bread. The aroma made them salivate until Andi finally broke down and bought them each one.

"Now we're down $10, and we haven't sold a single cupcake yet," Rachel complained.

She called out to the hundreds of people who packed the fairgrounds, and her face hurt from smiling, but despite her efforts, their booth was humiliatingly ignored.

"Maybe people don't think cupcakes go with crab or wine," Andi suggested.

Rachel's gaze drifted over to Gaston's setup. His booth was located in the corner, diagonal to their left. He looked up, caught her watching him, and smirked. His booth had a line thirty people long. Some of them backed up to the end of their cupcake table, all because he was serving crab chowder in fresh-baked bread bowls.

"Got to hand it to him," Rachel said, her spirits sinking. "Gaston has a smart marketing plan."

Andi nodded. "His success is in the presentation."

"He's slanted his product toward the venue, while we didn't." Rachel chewed on her lower lip. "Maybe we should have decorated the cupcakes to look like crabs."

"Maybe it wasn't such a good idea for us to come," Andi said and winced. "How much did this booth cost us?"

Rachel didn't even want to think about it. Thinking about money made her think about her grandfather. "We'll get some sales."

But by six o'clock that evening they'd sold only a few dozen cupcakes, not enough to cover a third of the cost. Rachel wondered what would happen the other two days of the festival. Would it be worth coming back? Since they'd already paid, they had no choice.

Andi glanced at her watch. "Time for me to pick up Mia from the babysitter's. Are you sure you'll be okay here by yourself?"

"Go ahead," Rachel replied. "We're dead here anyway. And someone has to stay in the booth till the end."

Her feet were tired from standing all day. The chatter from the crowd droned in her ears, giving her a headache. By the time she could leave and walked out to the parking lot, she was emotionally weary as well. She couldn't wait to get home and ... what was going on? Why was her car hooked up to the back of a tow truck? Her heart leaped into overdrive, and despite her aching feet, she ran toward it as fast as she could.

"Wait!" she shouted, waving her hands.

The tow truck driver gave her a quick glance and moved even quicker. Jumping into the cab, he started the engine.

"Where are you taking my car?"

"Ask the bank that gave you the car loan." He pulled away before she could respond.

Her chest caved in, making it hard to breathe. She'd been two months' late on her car payment, but she didn't think she was in danger of having it repossessed. And how did they know she was at the festival? She scowled. Either someone had blabbed, or the tow truck driver just didn't have many places to look. One of the unfortunate "benefits" of living in a small town.

She reflected back to the day she'd handed her car payment money to her mother to cover some of her grandfather's medical bills. She'd thought she could live without a car if she had to. Now she wasn't so sure.

"How am I going to get home?" she said out loud to no one in particular.

An elderly man wearing the yellow vest of a festival worker pointed to the dozens of school buses taking festivalgoers to various drop-offs around town.

Take a bus? She sighed. Better that than call Andi to come back out to get her. She was probably already putting Mia to bed, and there was no one else she could call. Her mother was never available. Kim had no car. Jake was away for the weekend. Guy didn't have his license due to a past DUI. And her cop friend, Ian Lockwell, was on duty.

Slinging her purse over her shoulder, she headed toward a yellow school bus, climbed the steps, and found a seat in the crowded reaches of the back.

She loved her red Mustang. It was a cool car, even if

it was dented and she couldn't afford a new one. Red was vibrant and an eye-catcher.

But the payments had been steep for her tight budget. The truth was, she was better off without the car. She'd felt guilty keeping it while her mother worked two jobs to cover her grandfather's medical bills. Now the matter was resolved for her.

She took her iPod from her purse, put on the connecting earbuds, and cranked up the volume to muffle the loud, boastful chatter of the obnoxious fairgoers who had drunk one too many samples of wine. They were having their own party, giggling, laughing, shouting at the people walking down the sidewalk as the bus stopped to drop people off at various locations. She hoped the bus would circle back into the heart of downtown Astoria soon, but she knew she had to be patient. Each bus had an assigned route. Rachel found it hard to keep her eyes open. She dozed off again and again only to wake with a start

"This is our last stop," the driver said over the intercom. "Please make sure you don't leave any articles behind. Pick up any trash you might have and deposit it in the garbage bag next to the exit."

The bus slowed to a halt and let off a hiss like a giant sigh of relief as twenty-five or more people stood up to get off, the noisy group that was having the party. Rachel was glad to see them go, but as they stepped off the bus, she realized she was the only one left. This couldn't be the last stop. The driver had to have misspoken.

She glanced out the darkened window and saw the

headlights from the bus illuminate the sign for the remote Fort Stevens Campground out by the ocean. She couldn't get out here. Fort Stevens was in the middle of nowhere.

And she wasn't much of a camper.

Chapter Four

> You don't love someone for their looks, or their
> clothes, or for their fancy car, but because they
> sing a song only you can hear.
>
> —Author unknown

RACHEL ROSE FROM her seat and walked up the aisle
toward the driver to admit her mistake. "I think I boarded
the wrong bus. I need to get back to West Astoria."

The driver turned around and gave her a big smile. "Happens every year. This is the Sturgeon bus," he said, pointing
to the sign above his head. "The Dungeness bus is the one
with the downtown route. On your way to the festival your
driver should have made you memorize '*I am a crab.*'"

"I didn't take the bus to the festival," Rachel replied,
"but I am feeling crabby."

"I'm sorry to hear that. I was hoping maybe you took the wrong bus on purpose."

His voice was warm and friendly, his smile disarming. Even in the dim light she could see he was handsome. If she weren't so tired, he'd definitely be someone she'd flirt with.

Instead, she frowned. "Why would I do that?"

"To see me," he said with a grin.

Was he flirting with her? Well, in that case, maybe she wasn't as tired as she thought.

"If I'd known you were this good-looking, I would have sat up front," she teased.

"If you did, I would have been distracted with thoughts of our upcoming date."

Upcoming date? *What date?* Was this his way of asking her out? Or did she meet him at a party several weeks back and forget to write his name down on her calendar?

Rachel stared at him, taking in his husky build, dark hair, strong jaw, and dazzling smile. She never would have forgotten to write down a date with him. She'd made the mistake of boarding the wrong bus, but maybe he'd also made a mistake. Mistaken her for someone else? She wouldn't let that deter her. "I'd love to go on a date with you. But right now I need to get home. I live at—".

"Two-three-three Franklin Avenue," he finished for her.

Rachel stiffened, fearing she may be alone in the middle of nowhere on an empty bus with a stalker. "How did you know?"

"Maybe I read your mind. Some magicians are known to possess that talent."

"*Mike?*"

He nodded. "I wondered how long it would take you to recognize me."

Relief surged through every part of her body, and she shook her head. This was the second time she'd thought the worst of him, and he'd surprised her. "I thought you were a stalker. How am I supposed to recognize you without the mask?"

"My voice?"

"Your voice did sound familiar, but I'm really tired and had a terrible day."

"Why don't you sit up here and tell me about it while I drive? I have to take this bus back to the school parking lot, but after that we can get my car, and I can take you home."

"Will you take me home, too?" The question came from behind them.

Rachel and Mike both turned their heads. An elderly woman, her white hair pulled back into a bun, poked her head over Rachel's shoulder. Rachel hadn't noticed her when she'd hurried up the aisle to approach the driver. The woman must have been hunched down, asleep in her seat, from too much wine. She could smell liquor on the old woman's breath.

"I'll call you a cab," Mike assured her.

"I'm Bernice Richards," she told them and pointed a finger at Rachel. "I saw you at the festival. You sell cupcakes."

"Yes," Rachel replied. "We have a shop in town, Creative Cupcakes."

Bernice's eyes fluttered, and she leaned her head back against the seat. "Let me know when we get there."

Mike called the cab service on his cell phone, and when they arrived at the bus lot, the yellow transport was waiting. Mike took the elderly woman's arm and helped her down the school bus steps so she wouldn't fall. Then, pulling his wallet out of his pocket, he paid the cabbie.

"That was sweet of you," Rachel told him as the cab pulled away.

Mike grinned. "She reminds me of my grandma, sweet as can be, but always into the cups on the weekends."

"Don't you think it's odd she's alone?"

"Lots of women come to these events and meet up in a group once they arrive. It's getting home that's the tricky part." He gave her a direct look. "Isn't it?"

"I'm glad I found you," Rachel said. "How did you get roped into working at the festival?"

Mike shrugged. "I heard they needed bus drivers, and since I have the qualified license and I'm between jobs, I thought I'd help out for the weekend."

He led her to his car, a black Grand Cherokee Jeep, and opened the door for her to get in.

"First a magician, now a bus driver, and Andi says that you make miniature models for movie sets. Seems you're very versatile," she teased. "What don't you do, Mike?"

"I don't stalk beautiful young women who happen to get on the wrong bus at the end of the night."

"Beautiful?" Rachel smiled on hearing that.

"And distraught. Like you need a hug more than anyone else in the whole world right now."

Rachel stared at him and nodded. Coming from another man, it would sound like a cheesy pick-up line. But the way Mike looked at her, even in the dim light, made her believe his compassion was real.

In any case, she didn't protest when he wrapped his arms around her and drew her close. His chest was warm. He made *her* feel warm, cocooned protectively in his embrace. And *secure*. Like her troubles didn't matter.

She wished he'd never let go, but a moment later he pulled back and started the car. She didn't usually show her emotions, but kept them hidden beneath her party girl smile. She must have slipped up tonight—maybe because she was so tired—for Mike to have seen through her.

He didn't ask what was wrong, but as Mike drove, Rachel found herself telling him anyway.

"The booth at the festival cost $400 for the weekend, and we barely broke a hundred bucks. No one wants cupcakes. All the people are interested in is eating crab and filling their wineglasses with samples from the local vendors. We need money, Mike. I need money. There are only two days left, and if I can't make a profit, Andi and Kim are going to hate me."

"Why would they hate you?"

"Because I'm the one who signed up for the festival, and instead of being Creative Cupcakes' 'stupendous' promotion manager, I'm feeling just plain *stupid*. Somehow I've got to come up with a way to sell more cupcakes."

"My brother has a booth at the festival this weekend, too. I used to work for him several years ago at his winery. He says first you need a good product."

Rachel nodded. "We have that. Our cupcakes are delicious."

"By themselves they might be delicious, but how do they taste after people have had several different glasses of wine?"

"I don't know," she admitted. "I never thought about it."

"Certain flavors of wine bring out a better taste in certain foods. One wine might go better with chocolate, while another might go better with vanilla. The key is to have customers taste the right combination so they'll think it's delicious enough to buy."

"If we served wine with the cupcakes, we could control what the customers taste before they sample our cupcakes, but all we have is cake."

"If I talk to my brother, he might be willing to sell some of his wine at your booth. Then you would have the right flavors, and he would have wine to sell in two locations."

"It's all about creative networking," she said, her heart beating faster. "Maybe Creative Cupcakes has a chance after all."

Mike shot her a sideways glance. "How are you serving the cupcakes?"

"On a napkin or small paper plate."

"What if you served them on something else, something unique? Something that ties in with the festival?"

"Like a . . . a wineglass?" As soon as the words left her

mouth, Rachel sat up straighter and took a deep breath. "We could serve them in a wineglass with a plastic spoon. But where would we get the glasses?"

"You could buy cheap plastic ones from the store, but a real glass would give the people a souvenir to take home, and they'd be willing to pay more for it. My brother and I used to buy from a glassblower on Commercial Street who sells wineglasses. You could ask if she'd be willing to cut you a deal if you buy in bulk."

Rachel slumped. "Put out more money?"

"What if you bring back what you don't sell? The glass shop owner might even want to come to the festival with you. You could sell your cupcakes, and she could sell the glasses to put them in. Except I'm not sure if people would want to carry the glasses around all day. Do you have a bag or something they could use to carry the glass home?"

"I saw a couple of people wearing a triangular fabric wineglass holder tied around their neck with a ribbon. The stem of the glass goes through a hole, and the cup part of the glass hangs in the material like a sling, allowing the customers to keep their hands free."

"Could you buy them from one of the other vendors?" he suggested.

"They are so simple that Andi, Kim, and I could make them."

"Do you know how to sew?"

Rachel laughed. "I do!"

She'd had to mend many of her own clothes in the past when her best outfits got a hole and she couldn't afford to buy new. Her mother had an old Singer sewing machine handed down to her from her mother.

"This is a great idea," Rachel said. "Thanks, Mike. You really are magnificent."

"You came up with most of the 'stupendous' ideas," he told her, his voice filled with amusement.

"But you helped me think."

"Sometimes two minds are better than one."

Or two hearts.

Mike parked his car in front of her house, turned off the engine, and opened his door to get out.

"What are you doing?" Rachel called over to him as she gathered her purse.

"Opening the door for you," he said coming around to her side, "and walking you up to the house."

No one had opened a car door for her in a long time. In fact, she couldn't *ever* remember a guy opening a car door for her. These days a gesture like that was seen only in movies.

He took her hand, and she smiled at him. "Thank you again for driving me home. I don't know what I would have done if the bus driver was a cranky old man who left me out at Fort Stevens overnight."

"You would have survived. It's very warm for the end of April, and I think you're a survivor, Rachel."

She stared into his eyes, stunned by his insight. She *was* a survivor. All her life she'd had to do what she needed to make ends meet, make friends, and continue on.

"I'll see you Wednesday night at six for our dinner date?" she asked.

His mouth curved into a grin. "What if I pick you up earlier, and we go back out toward Fort Stevens to spend the day at the beach?"

Rachel laughed. "Perfect. If we happen to get lost, at least I won't be alone."

Chapter Five

Alone we can do so little; together we can do so much.

—Helen Keller

INSTEAD OF GOING to bed that night, Rachel searched for her mother's sewing machine.

"I think it's in the back of the hall closet," her mom said, tapping her ceramic tea mug with her finger. "There might be some leftover fabric in there, too. Do you remember the floral print I used to make your Easter dress a few years ago?"

"Yes," Rachel exclaimed, her excitement erasing the sluggishness from her tired head. "The one with the pink-and-purple grape leaf design? I loved that dress. I wish it hadn't faded."

"You got quite a bit of wear out of that one." A brief flicker of a smile lit her mother's face but disappeared with a quick glance at the clock. "Wish I could stay up and help you, but you know—"

"You have work tomorrow," Rachel finished. "I know."

"We'll catch up with each other soon," her mother promised as she put her empty tea mug on the kitchen counter.

Rachel nodded. "Soon."

After her mother left, Rachel dug out the sewing machine, spent twenty minutes relearning how to thread the needle, then set to work cutting and stitching the floral fabric. Her mother had been right. Four yards of the grape leaf print remained, almost enough for another Easter dress. Definitely enough for two hundred three-by-three inch double thickness triangles. She also found several large spools of brand new ribbon in assorted colors. Each wineglass holder took only a couple of minutes to make. The main goal was to secure one side of the triangle to the other, not a huge project. She'd sewn harder patterns before. She'd just never had to stitch together *so many*.

Early the next morning she arrived at the cupcake shop in a predawn daze. She'd had no sleep, but, hey, she did have over two hundred triangle holsters.

"You sew?" Andi cupped her hand over her mouth but couldn't cover her surprise.

"I'm not Martha Stewart or Suzy Homemaker, but I can stitch together two pieces of material—yes."

"Rachel the seamstress." Kim laughed. "Who would have thought?"

"Don't tell anyone," Rachel warned. "It will ruin my image."

"We wouldn't want anyone to know that Rachel, the popular party girl, is actually a 'plain Jane' in disguise," Kim teased.

"There's nothing plain about Rachel," Andi said as she stocked the display case with a fresh batch of lemon–blueberry cupcakes. "Right, Rach?"

Rachel hesitated, and a cold, prickling sensation crept up her spine. "I hope not."

Kim pointed to the pile of stitched fabric triangles. "What do we do with these?"

"We need to sew ribbons on each end to turn them into necklaces the customers can wear," Rachel instructed. She held up the first one she'd finished as an example and put it around her neck. "See? I can carry a wineglass with no hands. The perfect souvenir after customers eat their cupcake. They can use the glass to taste wine at all the winery booths."

"Only problem is we don't have wineglasses," Andi said, flicking the switch to start brewing a pot of coffee.

"Kim and I are headed to the glassblower's studio now," Rachel told her. "You concentrate on making the rest of the cupcakes."

"Wait till you taste this new batch." Andi smiled and waved a hand toward the kitchen. "I created a new recipe."

"You didn't stick crab in the batter, did you?" Rachel asked, scrunching her nose.

Andi laughed. "No, of course not. This is my new creation for the Romance Writers group called a Recipe for Love. It contains bittersweet chocolate, chocolate chips, and whipped cream, and it's topped with a Hershey Kiss."

"Sounds good," Rachel replied. "I bet they buy a ton of them."

Andi wriggled her eyebrows. "That's the plan."

"The Lonely Hearts Cupcake Club might need the 'Recipe for Love,' too," Kim added.

Rachel reached beneath the counter, pulled out the Cupcake Diary, and wrote: Recipe for Love. "I might need that recipe myself," Rachel mused.

"We could all use a little more love," Andi assured her.

RACHEL AND KIM borrowed Andi's car, followed Mike's directions, and drove to the glass shop. They would have taken the Cupcake Mobile except neither one of them knew how to drive a vehicle with a clutch, a problem they would have to deal with later.

When Rachel stepped through the door of Astoria Glass Art, her gaze was drawn to the fabulous array of color adorning the walls, the tabletops, the shelves. There were glass sculptures, fluted bowels, vases, trays, candleholders, ornaments, beads, jewelry, and . . . wineglasses.

Kim walked toward a table of blue glass flowers with intricate petals and leaves. "This is amazing. Do you see how the glass is pulled and twisted?"

"Looks like a stretched piece of blueberry taffy," Rachel said, keeping her distance from the all-too-fragile pieces.

"I wonder if I could create something like this for the tops of our cupcakes using crystallized sugar and water."

"If you did, the cupcakes would be too pretty to eat," Rachel told her. "But you might win first place in an art show."

"I'm going to do it," Kim vowed, her green eyes lit with resolve as she turned around.

A woman in her midthirties with a sandy blond pony-tail walked toward them. "Can I help you?"

Rachel nodded. "Are you the owner?"

"Yes. Danielle Quinn."

Rachel thought the idea of asking the glassblower for help seemed logical when she'd talked with Mike. Now she hesitated, and felt self-doubt creeping in. "I . . . uh . . . we . . . are the co-owners of Creative Cupcakes on Marine Drive, and we have a booth this weekend at the Crab, Seafood, and Wine Festival."

Danielle rolled her eyes. "Twenty thousand people are expected to attend this year. The traffic through town has been horrible. It wouldn't be so bad if they came in my shop and bought something, but most of them are only interested in wine, not the glass."

"Which is why we're here," Rachel told her. "We would like to sell our cupcakes in wineglasses to encourage more sales."

"You're here to buy my wineglasses?" Danielle asked, her expression eager. "How many do you need?"

"We can't afford to buy them," Rachel said, shaking her head.

The glassblower put her hands on her hips and

scowled. "You don't expect me to donate them for free, do you?"

"What if we sell them for you at the festival?" Rachel suggested.

"No, this isn't going to work. I don't even know you." Picking up a pair of pliers and a long metal blowpipe, she walked toward the electric furnace at the back of the shop.

"But you know Mike Palmer and his brother, Tristan, from the Grape Mountain Winery," Rachel said, following her. "They highly recommended your work."

"They did?" Danielle paused, then took two steps back. "When did you speak to them? What did they say?"

Rachel smiled with the satisfaction of every performer who knows exactly when they've hooked an audience. "I spoke to Mike last night, and he said his brother would work with us and sell his wine along with our cupcakes. He said Tristan thinks your glassware is the best."

"He did?" The glassblower drew in her breath. "And you said Tristan will be there?"

"Yes, he has his own booth but will keep popping over to supply ours. Mike said you might want to come to the festival and sell your glasses with our cupcakes and Tristan's wine."

Kim nodded in agreement. "We'll all be working *together*."

Rachel shot Kim a mischievous look for emphasizing the last word, but it worked. Danielle shut down the furnace, called in some helpers to man the glass shop, and prepared to join them at the festival.

"If Tristan will be there, then so will I," she declared. "When do we start?"

ANDI, RACHEL, AND Kim drew straws and Andi lost, so while Andi stayed behind to operate Creative Cupcakes, Rachel and Kim went to the festival with Danielle. Unlike the day before, the second day of the festival spun sales around in all three directions. The cupcakes, the wine, and the wineglasses were an instant hit.

"This champagne pear cupcake is the best I've ever tasted and goes great with this dessert wine," one woman commented, pointing to the Grape Mountain Winery bottle.

"What a clever idea to serve cupcakes in a wineglass with a spoon," another woman blurted. "I want one."

A third woman in their group was jostled by the swarming crowd behind her, and the wineglass she'd been using slipped through her fingers.

The sound of the glass shattering on the ground drew the attention of other festivalgoers, who all stopped what they were doing and cheered.

The woman flushed, and she stepped forward and pointed to a chocolate Whoopie Pie cupcake in one of Danielle's wineglasses. "I want one because it comes with that ribbon holster to wear around my neck."

"Here, try this wine with that cupcake," Tristan said, pouring the woman a sample.

Before the group she was with left, they had spent over $100.

"This is wonderful!" Rachel exclaimed. "I can't wait to tell Mike."

"He said he'll stop in between bus runs," Tristan told her.

Rachel smiled up at him. Tristan was taller than his brother, less stocky, but had the same hazel eyes. Although she preferred his brother's looks, Tristan Palmer was a handsome man. It was apparent Danielle thought so, too.

As Tristan and Danielle flirted with each other, Rachel nudged Kim. "They remind me of Jake and Andi."

A twinge of loneliness pricked Rachel's emotions, but not enough to unload her feelings like those ridiculous women with lonely hearts who were meeting at Creative Cupcakes later that night.

Kim smirked. "I bet Tristan proposes before the festival is over."

"I saw Danielle enter her name into the drawing for a Hawaii vacation," Rachel confided. "Maybe if she wins they'll use it for their honeymoon."

Kim smirked. "I put Andi's name in the raffle. She really wants a warm island vacation."

"Andi already put her name in yesterday," Rachel said with a grin. "She also put in a ticket with my name, your name, and Jake's."

THE REMAINDER OF Saturday was swallowed up by a sea of people waiting to be served. Rachel, Kim, and Danielle couldn't hand out the cupcake glasses fast enough. The line grew longer each hour and picked up where it left off the next day. By the time Sunday evening came, Rachel was ready for the festival to be over.

She wasn't the only one. Gaston stomped toward their booth as they were closing, his dark expression contrasting with his white pastry chef's uniform.

"There were so many people here," he said, lifting his cleft chin, "you were bound to sell some. People come to the festival to taste samples. Now that they've tasted yours, I doubt they'll ever buy from you again."

Rachel wished she still had the wooden block she'd used during lunch to crack open crab legs so she could throw it at him. She knew better than to let her Irish temper flare in public, but her exhaustion had worn down her defenses. "Creative Cupcakes will continue to flourish, no matter what you say or do, so why don't you go back to your puff pastry?"

She was about to say more, but Kim put a hand on her arm.

"Don't waste your breath," Kim murmured. "His ego is as inflated as the hat on his head, but he's harmless. There's nothing he can do to us."

Rachel wanted to believe her, but she didn't trust that Gaston's words were only empty threats. He meant to sabotage their reputation, and as Creative Cupcakes promo manager, she'd be on her guard.

Chapter Six

We come to love not by finding a perfect person,
but by learning to see an imperfect person
perfectly.

—Sam Keen

RACHEL'S CELL PHONE chirped, and she took it out of
her pocket to glance at the caller ID above the incoming
number.

It was Mike.

She opened his message and read, *What would you
do if you had to choose between a million dollars and a
million kisses?*

Rachel smiled to herself. She'd been texting back and
forth with Mike all morning, each time answering crazy,
off-the-wall questions. She punched in her reply, *LOL. I'd*

take the money and run. You never said who the kisses would be from.

A few minutes later he texted back. *U R right. Could have been the Prince of Pastry or the tattoo artist next door 2 your shop.*

Rachel stifled a groan, her fingers pressing the keyboard on her phone as fast as they could. *Ugh to both. But the tattoo artist is a good friend.*

She hit "send" and waited for his next message. A moment later her cell phone buzzed, and she touched the "open" button on the message screen.

What if it were me?

Rachel stared at the words and pursed her lips. She typed back *I don't know how you kiss* and hit "send."

She congratulated herself on a smart answer as she walked down the street to the cupcake shop. When she arrived, she got another return text from Mike.

We could remedy that.

RACHEL WAS SINGING softly, thinking of her upcoming date with Mike that afternoon as she sat in front of her laptop at one of Creative Cupcakes' back tables. She looked up Mike's profile online, read all the newspaper clippings of his miniature models used in past films, and finally turned her attention back to her job.

First she posted photos and quick recaps on their success at the Crab, Seafood, and Wine Festival on their website, Facebook, Twitter, and a half dozen other promotional sites. Then she searched for the name Creative

Cupcakes on the Internet and found at least ten different blogs and review sites claiming their cupcakes left customers dissatisfied.

One reviewer stated, "Creative Cupcakes uses inferior ingredients, the cupcakes taste several weeks' old, and I saw a cockroach while waiting for the slow service girl to fill my order."

"This can't be right!" Rachel showed the review to Andi and Kim.

"Each blog and review uses the same phrases," Kim said, pointing out certain lines here and there. "I bet the same person wrote all of them."

Rachel scowled. "I bet it was Gaston."

Andi agreed. "Look at the ad alongside the review, for Hollande's French Pastry Parlor."

Rachel scrolled down the page, and a full-screen image of Gaston Pierre Hollande came into view. In his hands he held a book titled *How to Keep Your Bakery from Going Bankrupt*.

"He wrote a book?" Andi demanded.

"On sale now for only thirty bucks," Kim said, sounding like a commercial. "Who would pay that much? Avoiding bankruptcy is as simple as *not* buying his book."

A horn blasted from the street outside, and all three of them turned their heads, rose from their seats at the table . . . and gasped.

"His face is on the side of the bus!" Andi exclaimed, her voice rising. She walked closer to the window. "And on the billboard across the street."

Kim joined her. "I see him on the side of that yellow

taxi, the poster in the window of the gas station, and on the flyers those people are handing out on the sidewalk."

Rachel's legs trembled as she stood up, walked across the shop, and opened the front door. As she took in the new landscape, she thought it a miracle there wasn't a sign reading WELCOME TO THE WORLD OF GASTON.

How could they compete against such an aggressive promo campaign? She shut the door on him and took a deep breath, her mind reeling. She should have continued her education after high school. She should have gone to college for marketing or multimedia communications.

"Someday we'll have a golden trophy like Gaston claims he has," Andi said, her expression tight. "A cupcake trophy with a great big number one on top. Creative Cupcakes will win cupcake contests all over America."

Rachel turned and snapped her fingers. "What are we waiting for? Let's challenge him to a cupcake contest, like *Cupcake Wars* on TV, and offer the winner a magnificent trophy. I doubt Gaston would be able to resist, and we'll settle once and for all who's number one in this town."

"Yes," Andi agreed, her eyes wide. "But where?"

"The Astoria Sunday Market opens May twelfth, less than two weeks from now," Kim offered.

"Bake outside?" Andi asked.

"We can run extension cords and bring tables, mixers, and portable convection ovens." Rachel took the newspaper from the counter and waved it in the air. "If Jake can get the *Astoria Sun* to give us coverage, we may even pick up some sponsors."

"Jake!" Andi rushed to the television Jake had set up

in the corner. "He's on in twenty minutes. The local network is filming a segment on the newspaper and asked him for an interview."

"I can pay a visit to Hollande's French Pastry Parlor, throw down the challenge, and be back before Jake steals your undivided attention," Rachel promised.

True to her word, she returned to the cupcake shop with five minutes to spare.

"Well?" Kim asked. "What did he say?"

Rachel imitated the way Gaston Pierre Hollande had rubbed his hands together. "He can't wait."

MIKE MET RACHEL at the cupcake shop at noon. He was dressed in jeans and a blue plaid short-sleeved shirt over a white tee. His hair waved back from his face as if recently combed. And the smile on his face made her eager to go out and have a little fun.

"See you later," she called over her shoulder to Andi and Kim as she ditched the pink apron she wore over her blue-and-white sundress. Grabbing a jacket to protect her against the cool Oregon wind and her beach bag filled with necessities, she followed Mike out the door.

"You look great," he told her.

Tossing her red curls over her shoulder, she replied, "So do you."

Typical first-date conversation. Rachel smiled. She loved the thrill of discovery associated with first dates, but this one felt different. She'd been texting back and forth with Mike so many times over the last twelve days she felt as if she already knew him. There was an added intimacy to the usual words, and it threw her off guard.

He opened the door for her to climb into the Jeep and took a small bouquet of flowers off the seat. "Do you know what today is?"

She hesitated. "Wednesday, May first."

"May Day." He placed the ribbon-tied stems in her hands. "These are May Day flowers."

Rachel breathed in the deep fragrance of the tiny pink and white petals as she and Mike got in the car and he started the engine.

"In some parts of the United States," Mike said, driving toward their coastal destination, "a person sometimes fills a small basket with flowers or treats and leaves them on another person's doorstep. Then the giver knocks on the door and runs away."

"I never heard of this tradition. Why does the giver run away?" Rachel asked.

"So the person who receives the flowers can try to chase after and catch the fleeing giver."

"And if they do?"

"A kiss is exchanged." Mike turned his head, gave her a quick glance, and grinned.

Warning bells rang in her head as she grinned back, and her pulse kicked up a notch. Her suspicions had been right.

This wasn't going to be an ordinary first date.

AT LOW TIDE, the wide expanse of sand near Fort Stevens State Park seemed to stretch to eternity. The scene reminded Rachel of one of Kim's paintings of a pale dirt road that narrowed until it traveled off the page, leaving its destination to the beholder.

Mike took her hand, and the wind propelled them forward. The crashing waves of the Pacific Ocean lay on one side, the rolling dunes topped with tuffs of billowing green sea grass lay on the other. Tucked in between, the beach was a haven for seabirds and seclusion.

Mike lifted his camera and took a picture of the iron whalebone remains of the *Peter Iredale* shipwreck. "Back in 1906 this ship had four masts, was 285 feet long, and weighed 2,075 tons, too heavy to pull out of the sand when it ran ashore. Now it stays here stuck on the beach, a reminder of all the thousands of other vessels in the Graveyard of the Pacific."

"My grandfather told me twenty-seven crewmembers and two stowaways were rescued," Rachel said, thinking of the many times he'd brought her to this spot. "I always dreamed what it would have been like to be one of those stowaways."

"Hollywood is filming a movie about the shipwreck, and the two stowaways are the main characters," Mike told her. "Maybe you should audition for the part."

Rachel ran into the rusted bow and stuck her head through one of the many window-like openings in the metal framework. "Rachel Donovan, actress extraordinaire, playing the part of a *stupendously* charming stowaway living an enchanted life at sea."

Mike snapped a picture of her and then lowered the camera and let it hang from the strap around his neck.

"Your life hasn't been enchanting as Rachel living in Astoria?"

She stiffened. "Why do you say that?"

Mike walked closer and looked straight into her eyes. "Something in your voice sounded like you might be unhappy."

"Me, unhappy? I'm never unhappy." Rachel looked away, studied the round bolts in the metal framework around her, and turned back to meet his gaze once again. "Truth?"

Mike smiled. "Always."

"Instead of enchanted, sometimes I feel like my life is a shipwreck."

"With only the necessary bolts and framework holding you together?"

Rachel nodded. "How do you know?"

"Aaah, the illusion is always so much more fascinating than the real story, isn't it?" he asked, but the humor in his voice didn't reach his eyes. "When I was young my family was dealt a series of sudden deaths, and I found the best way to cope was to perform magic tricks to lighten the mood. Thus I donned the mask and became Mike the Magnificent."

Rachel turned around and rested her back on the edge of the ship. "You found it's easier to hide behind a mask?"

"We all wear masks, whether we see them or not, don't we?" His gaze locked on to hers. "But I've learned opening up to others and being myself is more fun than magic tricks."

Rachel disagreed. She thought his magic tricks were

enchanting. But she didn't argue. Instead, she admitted, "My family . . . isn't all there either."

Mike moved forward, sandwiching her between his husky body and the hull. He brushed a finger along her cheek and gave her a deep, penetrating look.

"I'll show you my real face if you show me yours," he said, his voice barely audible against the churning clap of another wave.

Rachel shoved the meaning of his words aside. All she wanted to do at that moment was kiss him. As he built a sand castle of the original *Peter Iredale* showing his expertise in creating precision models for movie sets, all she wanted to do was kiss him. And after they ate a picnic lunch on the sand dunes, all she wanted to do was kiss him.

But darn it, all Mike did was continue to romance her with his sweet talk, sweeter smile, and sweet yet disturbing way of looking right into her soul. He was so sweet, maybe she'd name a cupcake after him *after* she tasted his kiss. She only hoped the anticipation wouldn't be followed by a letdown. She had more than enough of those on her plate.

THEIR FIRST DATE included a mouth-watering dinner at the new surf-and-turf restaurant located in the old Bumble Bee Hanthorn Cannery on pier 39. Then Mike drove her home, opened the car door for her to get out, and walked her to the front door. He held her hand, and she turned to face him, certain she'd finally get a kiss.

"Today was fun," he said. His lips twitched into a half grin as he held her gaze.

"I had a good time," Rachel replied and tilted her head ever so slightly upward. Ready. Oh so ready.

"See you tomorrow?" he asked.

Rachel hesitated. If she saw him tomorrow, their two-date relationship would be over too soon. "How about next week?"

A flicker of mixed emotions crossed Mike's face, but it came and left so fast, she couldn't tell if he was disappointed, delighted, or undecided. She leaned closer, parted her lips, and squeezed his hand. In return, Mike pulled his fingers from hers and stepped away.

"Until next week then," he said, his eyes searching hers.

Wasn't he going to kiss her? Why wouldn't he kiss her? She thought they got along great. Didn't he feel the same way? Maybe she should have agreed to see him tomorrow. Maybe then he would have taken her in his arms and kissed her.

Rachel's stomach tightened. *I can't believe this.*

"I might be free tomorrow," she said, digging her toes into the tips of her shoes. "Call me."

"I will," Mike promised and turned to leave.

Ready to burst like a baked potato left in the oven too long, she closed the door and heaved a sigh. Her grandfather and his visiting nurse sat in the living room.

"By golly, will you look at that red hair!" he exclaimed. "I knew a girl with red hair once. Can't remember her name."

"Rachel?" the nurse prompted.

"No, not Rachel." He frowned. "Someone else."

The doorbell rang, and Rachel reopened the door, hoping Mike had come back. Maybe he decided he couldn't leave without giving her a kiss after all.

But no one was there. She looked around the driveway and neighboring yards. Then she looked down and noticed the basket of pink and white flowers on the front step, the same type of May Day flowers Mike had given her earlier when he told her the legend of . . .

She gasped, realizing Mike hadn't kissed her because he wanted to give her a choice. If she wanted a kiss, she'd chase after him. If not, she'd leave the door closed.

She sprang down the steps and rounded the corner of the house. He wasn't hard to catch. Mike spun around and laughed, his eyes gleaming with mischief. "I didn't think you were coming."

Her heart pounded. "I couldn't resist."

"See if you can resist this," he said, and with a grin, he leaned his mouth down to hers.

Chapter Seven

Love is always open arms. If you close your arms about love, you will find that you are left holding only yourself.

—Leo Buscaglia

LATE THE NEXT day Rachel stood beside Mike on the sidewalk in front of the parked Cupcake Mobile. Kim had finished painting a giant pink frosted chocolate cupcake on the side of the vehicle with three swords and their borrowed *Three Musketeers* logo, "All for one, one for all!"

Andi stood opposite them, her hands on her hips. "Rachel, it was your idea to get the truck."

"Yeah, but I didn't think I'd be the one who would have to drive it."

Kim balked. "Don't look at me; I doubt my feet would even reach the pedals."

"Well *I'm* not the only one who's going to drive this thing," Andi argued. "What we need is a delivery boy."

Mike grinned. "I could drive."

Rachel gave a start and turned her head toward him. "What do you mean?"

"I've been between jobs the last few months, taking on different paying gigs to float me until the next big paycheck," Mike told them. "I'd be happy to drive the truck and deliver cupcakes to your clients."

"W-work for us?" she stammered.

Andi clapped. "Oh, Mike, that would be great."

"Super great," Kim echoed and nudged Rachel with her elbow. "Don't you think so, Rachel?"

"Yes," Rachel said, forcing a smile. "Great."

Except . . . well, what about her two-date rule?

Andi and Jake had spent time together before their first official date. She supposed seeing Mike day to day in a nonpersonal capacity wouldn't count as a date for her either. She could do it. She was strong. Not like those women from the Lonely Hearts Cupcake Club.

After her second date with Mike this afternoon, she'd restrict their relationship to casual contact, and it would all be okay. Yes, she was sure everything would work out fine. Absolutely 100 percent perfect.

"Are you ready?" Mike asked, jingling his car keys.

"Yes," Rachel said and gave him a smile. "Always."

Two days later the Saturday Night Cupcake Club streamed through the front door of Creative Cupcakes and headed toward the party room.

Rachel eyed each of them, trying to decipher why they'd be rejected from the male population, why they had nothing better to do on a Saturday night than eat cupcakes with other dateless women.

Maybe because they'd *turned down* a date with a handsome man. That possibility had never entered her mind until she'd turned down Mike's offer to go to the movies minutes before they arrived.

Guilt shot through her entire body as she recalled the look upon his face. He hadn't been happy. And now . . . well, neither was she.

After mixing up a batter of peppermint mocha cupcakes, she drew close to the party room door and listened in on the women's conversation. One woman cried, saying that her boyfriend had left her. Another woman moaned that she was single and hadn't found anyone to fall in love with. A third had eaten chocolate to deal with her failing marriage, gained a lot of weight, and now didn't think anyone else would want her because she was fat.

Rachel pressed her lips together and shook her head. There was no way she'd ever humiliate herself in front of a bunch of other dateless women and wallow in self-pity. That's what it was, a big pity party. They each thought they needed a man, or help getting a man, when what they really needed was some mental help. If they really wanted a date, why didn't they go to a local hangout to meet someone? There were plenty of people over at the Captain's Port drinking, eating, and singing karaoke.

Instead, the women dragged their lonely hearts in here, where they devoured Andi's new Recipe for Love chocolate cupcakes and distributed Kleenex. *Pathetic.*

She spotted a book sticking out of a canvas bag on the floor and leaned her head in further. Was that Gaston's book, *How to Keep Your Bakery from Going Bankrupt*? No, but the covers were similar.

"Yoo-hoo, you there with the red head. Remember me?"

Rachel lifted her gaze to the woman with white hair beside the book bag who was waving to her. Bernice Richards, the little old lady from the festival bus?

"Come sit by me," Bernice called, "and join the group."

Rachel shook her head. "I can't. I've got work to do."

"I met a very handsome man at the festival last weekend, but he was too young for me and only had eyes for that pretty redhead," Bernice said, pointing in her direction. "What is your name, Pumpkin?"

If there was a single name Rachel hated as much as "the Sunkist Monster," it was "'Pumpkin."

"Rachel," she corrected, leaning her head into the doorway again. "My name is Rachel."

"What is your last name?" Bernice insisted. "A name isn't complete without both a first and last name."

"Donovan," Rachel answered. "Rachel Donovan."

"I knew a Lewis Donovan once." The old woman's eyes glistened, and her face took on a rosy glow. "He was very handsome, too. Had the same red hair as Rachel."

Rachel left the doorway and walked into the room. "Lewis Donovan is my grandfather."

Bernice's eyes widened, and all the other women, of all different ages, looked at her with interest.

"He was my beau," Bernice said softly. "We met right after high school, and he took me on the most glorious picnics by the ocean. We'd talk about sweet nothings and walk for miles along the water. He was my first real love."

"What happened?" Rachel asked, sitting down beside her.

"I wanted to marry him, but his father didn't think I was good enough to be his wife and sent him off to college."

"No!" Rachel exclaimed. How could her great-grandfather have done such a thing? How could *anyone* do such a thing? Who were they to judge who was good enough? What did "good enough" mean, anyway? Who gave others the right to think they were superior and others inferior? Fury burned through Rachel's veins, and she took Bernice's right hand in her own as if she still needed comfort after all this time. "Tell me what happened."

"After three years of separation he met someone else and had redheaded babies like you." Bernice paused, and her eyes filled with concern. "How is he?"

"My grandfather has Alzheimer's," Rachel told her. "He doesn't remember much."

Bernice sighed. "I'm sorry to hear that."

Rachel couldn't help but wonder what would become of her and Mike. Would they become separated for all time like Bernice and Grandpa Lewy? Would she end up in the Saturday Night Cupcake Club, alone and withered with no one to love?

Her stomach clenched. She didn't want to be alone.

The front door jingled as it opened, and Rachel rose to greet the new customer only to find Mike coming in from his last delivery. His gaze met hers, held, and then he turned away.

"Mike," she said, her voice raspy, probably from too much small talk with Bernice.

He turned back.

"If you still want to go, I'd love to see a movie with you tonight."

NOT ONLY DID she break her two-date rule, but she busted it to pieces by seeing Mike nearly every second of every day over the next full week. Today they'd be working together at the Astoria Sunday Market and compete against Gaston for the title of Best Cupcake Shop.

Rachel, still in pajamas, entered the kitchen of her family's house, poured herself a bowl of cereal for breakfast, and noticed her mother getting ready for work.

"Mom, you can't work today," she protested, jumping out of her chair.

"Rachel, I have to."

"But it's Mother's Day, a day of rest. No way should you have to work today."

"You'll be so busy with your cupcake contest you won't even miss me," her mother replied.

"That's not true," Rachel told her. "I want you to be there."

"Andi, Kim, and your new boyfriend, Mike, will be there." Her mother grabbed her purse off the table and headed toward the door. "You don't need me."

"I *do* need you, Mom."

But her mother didn't hear. She'd already left.

THE BRILLIANT BLUE sky sparkled with sunshine, drawing a large crowd to the Sunday Market in the historic downtown district. The tables of vendors selling fresh flowers, honey, oysters, jams, lavender, pottery, chainsaw carvings, and a unique assortment of homemade crafts spanned four blocks from Marine Drive to Exchange Street.

A teenager sat on the curb strumming his guitar. A hand-printed sign next to his open guitar case said he needed money to buy a car. He already had several donations.

"I should have brought some of my paintings," Kim said, scanning the artisans.

"You'll be too busy baking to sell your artwork," Andi told her. "Did you call to put your watercolors in the gallery in Portland?"

Kim bit her bottom lip. "Not yet."

"I've printed up a full-color flyer advertising that your paintings are available for purchase," Rachel confided. "And after we beat Gaston in the cupcake contest, there will be more customers coming into Creative Cupcakes to see them."

Kim's face brightened. "Thanks, Rachel."

A band played on the music stage as Jake helped Mike unload the tables and bakery equipment from the back of the Cupcake Mobile. The ovens were already there, supplied by a local used appliance store. When everything was in place, there were two identical makeshift kitchens set up side by side.

The head of the Sunday Market approached a microphone on the stage. "Welcome to Astoria's first Sunday Market Cupcake Contest," he said. "This year we have Creative Cupcakes competing against Hollande's French Pastry Parlor."

Cheers rose as the crowd drew in to watch.

"Everyone take a slip of paper," he continued, "and at the end of two hours we will distribute samples from each shop. Vote for your favorite flavor, and the winner of the contest will take home this glorious golden trophy!"

The trophy had been set up on a pedestal between the two kitchens, and Rachel caught Gaston staring at it.

Both bakery teams immediately set to work. While pouring ingredients into the large mixing bowls, Andi found herself mesmerized by the sparkle of diamonds.

"Did you see the ring on that woman's finger?" Andi drew in her breath. "Three full carats at least."

"I didn't notice," Rachel said, hustling to mix the next bowl of cupcake batter.

"How could you not?" Andi continued. "The shine sent a rainbow of color onto our baking table."

Rachel took Andi's left hand, touched the fourth finger, and smirked. "Gee, Andi, something seems to be missing here. What could it be? I'll have to mention this to Jake."

"Don't you dare!" Andi snatched her hand away and grinned.

Rachel held up her own bare hand. "I'll marry someday. I just need to find the right groom."

Andi nodded toward Mike as he approached. "Here he comes."

Rachel glanced at Mike and couldn't help but smile.

"I brought you the extra ingredients you asked for," Mike told them. "Is there anything else you need?"

"Rachel needs another kiss for good luck," Andi teased.

"Fine by me," Mike said and leaned over to place a quick kiss on Rachel's lips.

Beside the baking table, Mia and Taylor giggled and crooned, "Eww!"

Jake walked over to join them and made the two five-year-olds giggle once again when he kissed Andi.

"I did some research on Monsieur Hollande," Jake informed the Creative Cupcakes team. "He lied when he said he won the trophy on *Extreme Bake-off*. He got kicked off in the final week, and according to the press, he was *extremely* angry."

"That's why he's obsessed with being number one," Rachel said, dropping her voice so Gaston wouldn't hear.

"He set up a shop in Portland but couldn't outbake the city's competition, so he packed up and moved to Astoria," Jake added. "He thinks Creative Cupcakes and the other bakeries in town are an easy conquest."

"We won't be so easy to beat with these," Kim said, holding up one of her new crystallized sugar and water floral sculptures decorating the frosted top of a white chocolate–macadamia nut cupcake.

"It looks like glass," Rachel exclaimed, leaning in to take a closer look. "Like the blue glass flowers we saw in Danielle's glass shop."

Breaking apart, the group worked to finish baking the required 200 cupcakes by the two-hour deadline.

"We have only thirty minutes left," Andi reminded them as the contest drew to a close.

"Going as fast as I can," Rachel replied, pulling another batch out of the oven.

Mia called to Andi across the zoned off bake area, "Taylor said I took her candy, but I didn't. She took mine."

Taylor pulled Jake by the hand and came toward them.

"Taylor wouldn't lie," Jake told Andi.

Andi stopped icing the cupcakes and looked him in the eye. "Mia wouldn't lie either."

As their voices rose and the squabble continued, Rachel turned her head to find Gaston next to their table, where they had placed a large bowl of cupcake batter. He smiled and turned away.

Rachel walked toward the bowl and looked inside. Nothing looked wrong, but she figured she'd better be sure. Taking a spoon, she scooped some of the batter and lifted it to her mouth.

"*Ugh!*"

Andi turned toward her. "What's wrong?"

"Salt." Rachel scrunched her nose and wiped her tongue with a nearby towel, but the sharp taste remained.

"Did you mix up the ingredients?" Andi asked.

"No." Rachel shook her head and pointed to the label on the container of salt, which now had an uneven cap. "It wasn't me. I think it was Gaston. He dumped salt into the batter."

Kim came toward them and pointed to her watch. "Do we have time to make another batch?"

Andi shook her head. "Worse. We're out of ingredients."

Rachel called Mike over to them. "Can you go back to the shop and bring us the extra batter I put in the refrigerator?"

Mike nodded and dashed off to the Cupcake Mobile.

Ten minutes later he was back, bowl of batter in hand. Andi, Rachel, and Kim scooped the cream-colored mixture into the last tray and put it in the oven.

"Five minutes to ice and decorate these," Andi called when the cupcakes were finished baking.

Kim nodded. "Ready and waiting."

The announcer began counting down the minutes over the microphone, and Rachel held her breath. Her fingers had never worked so fast. She, Andi, and Kim plopped icing onto the last dozen cupcakes, spread the mixture with a knife, and finished placing Kim's sugar sculptures on the tops just as the final whistle blew.

Rachel narrowed her gaze at Gaston as the cupcakes were distributed and people placed their votes in the ballot box. He gave her a smug look, then turned to converse with his two helpers.

Members of the Astoria Fire Department had been chosen to count the votes, and after twenty minutes, the announcer stepped up to the stage and took the microphone in his hand.

"The winner of the contest is . . . Creative Cupcakes!" he exclaimed.

Gaston's face reddened, his forehead creased, and his hands balled into fists of rage. "This cannot be! What do you people know about quality cupcakes? No one can beat Hollande's French Pastry Parlor! The trophy should be *mine*."

"Sorry," Rachel told him, holding the trophy up for all to see. "Looks like you may need to move to another town if you want to be number one."

Gaston snarled. "I'm not going anywhere."

Chapter Eight

Ideas should be clear and chocolate thick.

—Spanish proverb

RACHEL LEANED OVER the shop counter and looked at
the notes she'd written in the Cupcake Diary. Her handwriting lacked its usual boldness, appropriately enough
since Creative Cupcakes lacked its usual sales. The contest at the Sunday Market hadn't helped. A week had
passed, and Rachel was afraid to show Andi and Kim the
latest receipts.

Mike came back from delivering a couple of dozen
cupcakes to a birthday party and sat on a stool opposite her.

"Having a bad day?" he asked.

Rachel looked up. Never had she met anyone who

could pick up on her moods so well. Most people bought the perky smile, laughter, and happy attitude act. Of course, when you spent as much time together as she and Mike had over the last couple months, your inner emotions were bound to show. A simple "I'm fine" wasn't going to cut it. Mike would know if she wasn't telling the truth.

"My grandfather's taken a turn for the worse," she said, forcing the words from her mouth. "He didn't say anything when I brought him his slippers last night, but I didn't think anything was odd until my mom told me this morning that he hasn't spoken in three days. There's an experimental treatment that might help him, but Creative Cupcakes isn't making enough money for me to help my mom with the finances."

"What about a window display to draw more people into the store?" Mike suggested.

Rachel glanced at the large front window. Sheer pink curtains framed the glass, and dozens of cupcakes in assorted colors sat on multilevel tiers.

She shrugged. "We have a window display."

"I keep imagining a four-foot detailed miniature model of the Astoria–Megler Bridge lined with cupcakes in the shape of cars."

"Ooh! That would be perfect! Tourists could look at the real bridge, turn around, and see the model in our window." Rachel sucked in her breath. "What if we have a sign saying, 'See more of Mike Palmer's models inside'? Then people will come through the door and have their noses assaulted by the strong aroma of fresh-brewed coffee and sweet, creamy, melt-in-your mouth cupcakes. They won't stand a chance. They'll have to purchase some to take home, and Creative Cupcakes will be a raving success."

Mike grinned. "Sounds like you've got it all figured out."

"With your help," she said, staring at his handsome face.

She picked up a pen to write the new idea down in the Cupcake Diary, and her hand accidentally brushed the pages backward. The words "Red carpet invites" jumped out at her. Of course! One of their original ideas for a promotion. Andi had been joking at the time, but, hey, why not?

"When could you have the window display ready?" Rachel asked, her voice trembling with excitement.

Mike took a moment to consider. "Next weekend?"

"Perfect," Rachel said. "I'll plan a promotion party with 'red carpet invites' for people to come see your models, and Creative Cupcakes will be the talk of the town."

She could already see the headlines in the *Astoria Sun*, drawing attention to their success. With Mike's models and her party planning, how could they lose? For Mike had already had his talents featured in the paper, and if there was one thing she was good at, it was throwing a great party.

THE ONLY DRAWBACK to Mike's model-building idea was the fact he'd had to cancel their date that night to start gathering supplies.

Rachel washed the beaters of the industrial mixer in the sink, wiped her wet hands on a dishtowel, and decided to approach Andi. They'd been so busy the last few months with the cupcake shop, they hadn't had a chance to hang out like old times.

"Would you like to go to the mall tonight?" Rachel asked. "We could go window shopping and make a wish list so when we get rich someday we know what to buy."

"Sorry," Andi replied. "Jake and I are taking the girls to see my father's new house in Warrington."

"Oh." Rachel smiled to mask her disappointment. "I'll ask Kim."

Andi hesitated. "Kim's going, too. It's my dad's birthday. But I'd love to go to the mall with you. Soon?"

Rachel's smile faltered when she heard that all-too-familiar word. "Sure," she said. "Soon."

The group of women entering the shop waved to her and asked her to join them: the Saturday Night Cupcake Club, or the Lonely Hearts Cupcake Club, as she, Andi, and Kim referred to them. Pathetic souls. Rachel took a look at their long, drawn faces and felt sorry for them. In fact, she felt so sorry for them, she served them a batch of Andi's Recipe for Love triple-chocolate cupcakes on the house. It was the least she could do. Some of the stories she overheard wrenched her heart.

"He said he didn't know who I was, that I never showed any emotion," one thirty-year-old woman told the group. "So he gave me a choice: open up to him about my feelings, or he'd go."

Rachel gasped. "What did you do?"

"I came here," the woman replied. "A chocolate cupcake is better than a smarty-pants old man any day."

"Didn't you love him?" Rachel asked, the question popping from her mouth before she had time to think.

The woman stared at her for several long seconds, and then her shoulders began to shake. It looked as if she wanted to say something when suddenly she nodded and burst into tears. Rachel joined the others who put their arms around her.

"We all make mistakes," Bernice said in a tone meant to soothe.

Rachel realized she might have made a mistake by misjudging the group. They were all here for each other when they needed support. That wasn't so bad, was it?

After the meeting, Bernice drew Rachel aside. "I've brought you something," she said and handed Rachel a tattered black-and-white photo.

The picture had been taken at the beach with the *Peter Iredale* shipwreck in the background, a young couple in front. The man looked familiar.

"Is that my grandfather?" Rachel asked.

Bernice nodded. "And me."

"Your hair was dark."

"Used to be red like yours a long time ago." She patted her white bun atop her head and smiled. "I was hoping you could show this photo to Lewis to see if he remembers."

Rachel took the photograph but didn't have the heart to tell her that Grandpa Lewy didn't recognize anyone. Not even his own granddaughter.

THE FOLLOWING FRIDAY Mike unveiled his exquisite model of the Astoria–Megler Bridge for Creative Cupcakes' promo party that night. Rachel's gaze followed the sweeping midair curve of the miniature ramp to the high steel girder, continuous truss, cantilever stretch with its two mint green triangular peaks, then down to the flat, open, low-water section leading across the Columbia River. The model bridge had two lanes, one going in each direction from Astoria to Point Ellice near Megler, Washington.

On the Oregon side, Mike had constructed a replica of Astoria, with the white *Queen of the West* paddle wheeler, the waterfront park, piers, the Maritime Museum, the hillside's famous Astoria Column, and a square brick shop on Marine Drive with a bright red door.

"Creative Cupcakes!" Rachel said, pointing. "Mike, I had no idea you were so talented."

"Don't you mean 'magnificent'?" he teased.

"Yes," she said, flinging her arms around his neck. "Mike the Magnificent."

"Magnificent enough to marry me?"

"Very funny." She laughed. "Now, be serious."

Mike kissed her and then looked around the interior of the shop and frowned. "What's all this?"

Rachel glanced behind her. "Decorations for the

party."

"They're . . . fancy."

Silver and gold streamers hung from the ceiling. Silver tiered trays held dozens of beautifully decorated cupcakes with gleaming candy pearls. White tablecloths covered every table, and shiny silver ice buckets held bottles of wine and champagne.

Kim marched toward her. "This isn't who we are at all. I told you not to go overboard. Andi, tell her."

Instead, Andi scowled and held up a handful of flyers. "What's this?"

"Release forms," Rachel replied.

Andi narrowed her eyes. "Release forms for what?"

"The party is going to be on YouTube," Rachel explained. "I thought about Gaston's reality TV show and figured we could do the same. I've arranged for a camera to film short, sporadic segments throughout the night."

"Where is it?" Kim asked, looking around.

"In the corner, hidden behind that fake tree," Rachel told her.

Andi and Kim glanced at the tree and then stared at her, as if shocked. Didn't they realize how much a video of a party like this could boost their shop's reputation?

"Why don't the two of you dress up for the party and wear something a little more stylish," Rachel suggested.

Kim glanced down at her black cap-sleeve shirt and jeans and pursed her lips. "You're the party girl, not me."

"I don't have any elegant dresses to change into," Andi complained. "And I had no idea you planned to turn the shop into a glitzy Hollywood extravaganza. How could you do this without talking to us about it first?"

"I wanted to surprise you."

"Oh, yeah," Kim said, her tone heavy with sarcasm. "We're surprised, all right."

Great. Now, Andi and Kim were mad at her.

Okay, she should have let them in on the plans. But Andi had been busy with Jake, and Kim had kept her nose stuck in her paintings most of the week. They'd left it up to her to make Creative Cupcakes a success. And a success it would be.

"Here they come," Rachel said and pasted on a dazzling smile as the guests began to arrive.

The glassblower, Danielle Quinn, and Mike's brother, Tristan, headed toward them hand in hand.

"I won the raffle for two tickets to Hawaii at the Crab Festival," Danielle announced. "But I can't use them because my brother is getting married that weekend in Ohio. If you want them, I can sell them to you cheap."

"Thanks," Kim said, "but I'm terrified to fly. Besides, I have my own trip to go on. Not far, but I'm traveling to Portland to display my paintings in my first art gallery show."

"I have no money right now," Rachel told her. "Every penny has to go to help my mom and my grandpa."

"I'll take them," Andi said in a rush. "Jake and I would love to go on vacation, and I've never been to Hawaii."

Rachel smiled and congratulated everyone else on getting everything they ever wanted. Danielle had Tristan. Kim had her art gallery show. Andi had her vacation with Jake. Life was wonderful, wasn't it? Perfect. Just *great*.

"The cupcakes are fabulous," one woman raved, latching on to her arm. "Are you the one who created these exquisite crystallized designs on the tops of each cupcake?"

"No," Rachel said, wishing she had. "That was done by Kim. She's the skinny one with the shoulder-length dark hair."

"Looking good, Rachel," a man she'd met at a friend's party the previous month called to her.

She glanced down at her glittery gold dress and then at the young man's Armani suit. "So are you, Gabe."

Rule number one at a party: learn everyone's names. Rachel smiled at him and turned to the throng of others waiting to speak to her.

"Lots of gorgeous guys here to help celebrate," another female acquaintance said, her tone appreciative. "Great going, Rachel. You've got it going on, girl."

"This place is the 'cupcake connection,'" Rachel told her. "The perfect place to meet and fall in love."

"Is that why we haven't seen you lately, Rachel?" asked another guy. "Have you fallen in love with someone?"

"Oh, no. I'm single and loving it," Rachel replied. Turning her head, she caught Mike's eye.

He didn't blink, didn't turn away, but looked straight at her. What had he wanted her to say? They'd never discussed the *L* word.

Then why did she feel so guilty?

Maybe because she was single and *not* loving it.

She hadn't been to many parties the past two months. She'd been busy working. But now as everyone flirted with her and she flirted back, the whole popular party girl persona she strived to keep up felt more unnatural than ever before.

Fixing her attention on the goal of promoting her party, she walked over to Caleb O'Neal. He worked with a local media crew, and they'd met when Jake had him install a security camera in the shop.

"Are we being recorded right now?" Rachel asked.

"Yeah," Caleb assured her. "It's on a timer, and I'll upload to YouTube as soon as the party's over."

"Make sure you film everyone having a great time," Rachel told him.

She walked toward the front window display by the model Astoria–Megler Bridge lined with cupcakes, and Mike joined her.

"Who was that?" Mike asked, nodding to Caleb.

Rachel smiled. The young tech guy was only twenty-two but looked much older, old enough to be considered competition. "Do I detect a hint of jealousy?" she teased.

Mike grinned. "I can't ask you to marry me if you're interested in someone else."

Rachel rolled her eyes. "Be careful how you joke with me, Mike Palmer. One of these times when you ask me to marry you, I might be tempted to say yes."

"Really?" Mike asked. "Then tell me, who's the techie?"

Rachel shrugged. "He's just a friend."

"Like me?"

"Rachel has lots of friends," a woman nearby interrupted. "She's friends with everyone, the friendliest person on earth."

"I think you've had too much to drink," Rachel told her.

"There's never too much to drink," the woman said and asked the crowd around her, "Am I right?"

"Right!" the people cheered.

Two months ago Rachel might have cheered with them. Tonight all she wanted was to kick them out of her shop. But she couldn't. Tonight she was filming the promotion video for Creative Cupcakes, the most hip, perfect party place in town.

"You didn't have to do this," Mike said, his face grim. "This isn't you. This isn't the Rachel *I* know."

"You're right. This was a mistake."

Mike gave her a solemn look. "The party? Or me?"

"Definitely not the party," Gabe said, dancing around with a wineglass in one hand, a rocky road cupcake in the other.

"I'll catch up with you later," Mike told her and backed away.

"Mike, wait," she called, but it was too late.

Other people were clamoring for her attention.

Suddenly, a loud shriek shot across the room. Rachel turned her head and saw a woman jump back and bump into the four-foot-high tiered cupcake display. The entire table of iced cupcakes tipped over and crashed on the floor.

Other people jumped back, and more screams erupted as everyone jostled this way and that, hopping from one foot to the other. Scream after scream pierced the air. Then the crowd parted, and a six-inch hairy gray animal ran straight across the middle of the floor.

"Rat!" someone cried out.

Rachel groaned. She'd wanted this Memorial Day weekend party to be memorable in a good way, but everything had turned terribly wrong, and this was the icing on the cake, pun intended.

She found Andi's and Kim's horrified faces in the crowd. Then like magnets they pushed through the screaming customers and drew together.

"How did a rat get in here?" Andi shouted.

"Through the front door?" Kim asked.

Beside them, their skinny, tattooed next-door neighbor began to sway.

"Have I ever told you I . . . I . . . have an extreme fear of rats?" Guy said, his eyes rolling back.

"Oh, no!" Rachel exclaimed. "Catch him!"

"The rat?" Kim asked, confused.

"Guy!"

Andi caught him on one side, Rachel on the other, and Kim tried to support him from behind.

"He's fainted," Andi said, her voice strained. "Put him down."

They let his limp body sag to the floor, and the rat ran right past him. Good thing he wasn't awake to see it.

Goosebumps rose on Rachel's arms and prickled her skin. She didn't like rats either.

Jake ran forward with an empty garbage can and threw it over the rat, but the rodent kept racing across the room, pulling the can with it.

The crowd shrieked even more, and everyone tried to

run out the front door in a mass panic. An old man fell to the ground and would have been trampled, but Mike pulled him to his feet just in time.

Rachel let out a sigh of relief. The man reminded her of Grandpa Lewy.

A siren grew louder as it approached, and she turned her head toward the window. "Did someone call the cops?"

Officer Ian Lockwell and his partner stepped inside. Mike must have slipped out while she and the others were giving their statements because Rachel didn't see him the rest of the night. Caleb slipped out, too, before she could stop him from uploading the video to YouTube.

And to add a final poke to the party, someone had stolen the golden cupcake trophy.

Chapter Nine

> When stressed, women eat ice cream, chocolate, and sweets because stressed spelled backwards is desserts!
>
> —Author unknown

RACHEL WOKE THE next morning after a restless sleep and sat at the kitchen table with Grandpa Lewy. Neither of them talked. Her gaze drifted to his. Was it possible he was feeling as down and depressed as she?

Reaching into her purse, she pulled out the black-and-white photograph Bernice had given her and slid it in front of him. Her grandfather didn't look at it, didn't move. He just continued to stare into space.

Her mother, however, glanced over his shoulder as she brought the coffee mugs to the table.

"Who's that?" her mother asked, squinting at the photo.

"Grandpa Lewy and his long-lost love, Bernice Richards," Rachel told her. "They met right after high school before Grandpa went to college. Last month I met Bernice on the bus coming home from the festival, and now she's a regular at the cupcake shop."

"Bernice Richards," her mother repeated, sitting down at the table with them. "I know that name. Your grandpa used to talk about her all the time after your father's mom died. He said it was misfortune that separated them. He loved your grandmother, but he always referred to Bernice as 'the one who got away.'"

Rachel thought of Mike and his pale, troubled expression the night before. She didn't want him to be "the one who got away" in her life.

"She had red hair."

Rachel jumped back in her seat with a start. She glanced at her mother, who had spilled her coffee, and then at her grandfather.

He was looking at the photo.

"Yes, Grandpa," Rachel prompted. "She used to have red hair like us."

"I was trying to remember her name," her grandfather said, his voice soft. "I kept seeing her face but couldn't remember her name."

"She remembers you," she told him.

"Bernice looked a lot like you, Rachel. Young. Smiling." Grandpa Lewy smiled, and suddenly his memories sprang forth like a rushing river. He told them every explicit detail of the day he and Bernice had met, the courtship that followed, the loneliness after his father separated them.

"She really loved me," he said, grinning from ear to ear.

"Rachel and I love you, too, Dad," her mother added.

He responded by telling more stories, stories of when Rachel's father met her mother and some of when Rachel was little. There was no telling how long his clarity would last, but for the moment, it was enough.

When Rachel looked across the table, she saw that her mother was crying. "Mom, are you okay?"

Her mother nodded. "It's a miracle."

"Miracles can happen."

Pushing back her chair, her mother stood up, came around the table, and hugged each of them. "Rachel, let's make a date to go out to lunch."

Rachel gave her a half smile and shrugged. Her mom meant well, but . . .

"I bought theater tickets," her mother continued, and going to the kitchen drawer, she pulled them out and waved them in the air as proof. "We can go to lunch before we watch the show."

Rachel stared at the tickets dated for the following week. "Where did you get the money?"

Her mother hesitated as she laid a hand on Grandpa Lewy's broad shoulder. "We don't have enough money for Grandpa's treatment. Not nearly enough. There's nothing I can do about that. But I can do something for someone else I love, someone I've been neglecting."

Rachel swallowed hard. "I forgive you."

"I know you do," her mother assured her. "But your grandpa has taught me that recognizing and loving each other is more important than working overtime. I don't want to lose you, too."

"You'll never lose me," Rachel promised, and as they hugged, Rachel thought of Mike. And Andi. Kim. Their cupcake shop.

She didn't want to lose any of them, but after her disaster of a party the night before—uploaded to YouTube for all the world to see—she doubted any of them would want anything to do with her for a long time. Maybe not ever.

Was it too much to ask for two miracles in one day?

RACHEL ARRIVED AT Creative Cupcakes determined to talk to them, but Mike didn't show up, and Andi and Kim avoided her the entire morning—except to make a few notable entries in the Cupcake Diary.

One note written in Andi's small typewriter print read, *"YouTube sensation, 10,000 viewers. Promotion guru throws heck of a party as rat is released."*

The word "rat" was crossed out with a giant *X*, and Rachel's name had been written above it in Kim's swirly handwriting with its cursive embellishments.

Andi and Kim both stayed in the kitchen and left Rachel to man the front counter. She hadn't realized what day it was until the Saturday Night Cupcake Club filed through to the back party room. Except it was only midafternoon. What were they doing here so early? Oops.

She'd missed it. A note in the Cupcake Diary stated they were coming in at three o'clock because it was Memorial Day weekend, and the holiday made them extra sad.

Great. The last thing she needed was to have to listen to another sob story. Loading a tray of Hidden Berry cupcakes onto a tray, she made her way toward them.

They were talking about loneliness. Rachel thought of Bernice and her grandfather, which led her to think of Mike and the beach. Would she spend the rest of her life stuck in the same lonely spot like the *Peter Iredale* shipwreck? The ship's captain had toasted his ship with these words: "May God bless you, and may your bones bleach in the sands."

She didn't want *her* bones to bleach in the sands. She wanted a life filled with possibilities, a life filled with love. Placing the tray down on a nearby table, she dropped into a chair.

"Rachel, what's wrong?" Bernice asked, hurrying to her side.

The other women gathered around, too.

Tears stung her eyes, and whether she liked it or not, she began to cry. "I've dated a string of men, one after the other, never going on more than two dates with any of them. I've been afraid to let anyone get too close, afraid they will see who I really am and not like me, not think I'm good enough. But I feel so alone, and I don't want to be alone anymore."

"You aren't alone, Rachel," one of the other women told her and put her arms around her shoulder to give her a hug. "We are here for you."

The others all nodded their heads and chorused their agreement.

"The worst of it," Rachel said, wiping her cheek with a tissue one of the women offered, "is that I fell in love with one of them. Mike Palmer. He's fun, talented, caring, and insightful. I've never felt this close or this vulnerable to anyone before. He sees into me, sees things I can't even see. Except I messed up last night, and I think he saw something he didn't like." Her throat constricted. "I know I did."

"We all have regrets," Bernice said, patting her arm.

"My grandpa Lewy hasn't recognized anyone for two months," Rachel told her. "We can't afford the treatment he needs, but this morning he saw your photo and remembered you. He remembered everything about you, remembered you loved him. That's the kind of love I'm afraid I'll never have."

The corners of the old woman's eyes grew moist, and another woman said, "We all share the same fear, Rachel."

"I've been hiding my fear behind an invisible mask of endless parties and fake smiles." She shook her head. "I don't want to wear a mask anymore, but I think it's too late. I think I lost him. Lost Mike. And lost Andi and Kim, my two best friends in the whole wide world."

"No, you haven't." It was Andi's voice.

Rachel looked past the crowd and saw her friends standing behind them. The other women let them through, and Andi and Kim drew in close to wrap their arms around her, too.

"You're still my best friend," Andi told her.

"And mine," Kim added.

Jake appeared in the doorway, gave everyone a big grin, and held up the cupcake trophy. "Look what Officer Lockwell found in Hollande's French Pastry Parlor."

"Gaston took it?" Rachel asked.

"He also released the rat," Andi informed her. "Your YouTube clip caught him standing by the shop's side door and releasing the thing from a cage. As a result, everyone we've talked to in Astoria plans to boycott his bakery."

Kim smiled and quoted their motto borrowed from *The Three Musketeers*, " 'All for one, one for all.' "

"I'm glad we don't have to worry about any more thieves," Rachel said and frowned. Didn't she set a plate of Hidden Berry cupcakes on the back table? Her gaze swung from the empty space to the outward swing of the front door, then back to the group.

"Nothing is going to tear us apart," Andi vowed, her voice firm. "Or you and Mike. You need to go after him and tell him how you feel."

Kim nodded. "I saw him down by the waterfront. If we move fast—"

"Wait," Bernice said and placed a handwritten check in Rachel's hand. "Take this for your grandpa's treatment."

Rachel gasped. "It's too much—"

Bernice shushed her. "I'm old and rich. Very rich. Now, go. And don't let anything stand in the way of true love."

"I won't," Rachel promised. And with the other women's promise to watch over the cupcake counter, and Andi and Kim by her side, she rushed out of the shop.

Chapter Ten

> To love a person is to learn the song that is in
> their heart, and to sing it to them when they have
> forgotten.
>
> —**Arne Garborg**

OUT OF BREATH, Rachel reached the waterfront walk. "I don't see him, do you?"

Andi shook her head. "No."

"He can't be far," Kim encouraged.

The sky was dark and churning and held the threat of a storm moving in. The wind whipped their hair back, and a foghorn blew somewhere in the distance. Then, appearing out of the gray landscape, the pale yellow-green-and-maroon restored 1913 Astoria Riverfront Trolley jingled as it came up the track and stopped in front of them.

"If we board the trolley, we can look for him along the whole two-and-a-half mile stretch," Andi suggested.

"Do you have a dollar for the fare?" Kim asked.

Andi looked in her purse. "I'm broke."

Kim's pockets came up empty. "So am I."

"I have some singles," Rachel offered, but when she opened her purse, all of the contents fell out on the ground.

Andi and Kim bent to help her scoop up her large array of lipstick, mascara, apple-blossom perfume, nail polish, hairbrush, keys, mints, and other miscellaneous items.

"We have to leave," the white-bearded conductor told them. "It's a holiday weekend, and we're on a tight schedule. You can catch the trolley on our next trip back."

"No, please wait." Rachel held up three singles. "I've got it."

Andi and Rachel took seats on one side, while Kim dropped onto a deep-polished wooden bench opposite them so they wouldn't miss Mike if he was on either side of the tracks.

The bell sounded, and as the trolley moved forward, the conductor began to recite its history. Rachel scanned the dozens of people they passed, but Mike was nowhere in sight.

"Up ahead the trolley goes over a stretch of water," the conductor continued. "We haven't had an accident yet, but be advised the person sitting next to you is your nearest floatation device."

Rachel prayed the trolley wouldn't fall into the water

this time either, but with her luck, she wasn't too sure. A few minutes later the trolley returned to dry land and stopped for a long line of people waiting to board. Not willing to waste any more time, she got up out of her seat.

"What are you doing?" Andi called, jumping up to follow.

"I can't wait," Rachel said. "I might miss him. I'll go the last stretch on foot."

As they hurried down the waterfront path, she feared she'd missed him anyway. They were almost to the end. The trolley was catching up to them, and Rachel moved into one of the three-by-six-foot railed, wooden deck cutouts to get off the tracks. Andi and Kim followed, and the trolley passed by and stopped a few yards ahead.

Rachel looked out over the wide mouth of the Columbia River, toward the red and green lights set to guide the ocean-bound ships in the right direction, and wished she had such a beacon.

She shook her head. "I've lost him."

A card swirled into the air in front of her, and she reached out and grabbed it. A Creative Cupcakes business card?

She spun around, and Mike, dressed in a suit and tie, stood in front of her, his dark hair ruffled and a bright smile lighting his handsome face. Rachel drew in her breath. He didn't seem to be unhappy with her at all. In fact, he seemed mischievously pleased, like he knew a secret she didn't.

Andi and Kim also wore huge smiles on their faces

as if they also knew something. What were they keeping from her?

"I was online less than an hour ago, replying to a job inquiry when I saw *you*," Mike said, his voice calm.

"Me?" Rachel asked. "From the video clip filmed last night?"

"No," he said with a grin. "From the video clip filmed *today*."

"Today? What do you mean *today*?"

"When you stood up and poured your heart out in the Creative Cupcakes party room, you were being filmed," Mike told her.

Andi nodded. "Caleb set the camera on a timer to film the same hour every afternoon and evening," she explained. "After the chaos at the party, he didn't turn it off, and someone must have knocked the lens because today it zoomed in on the party room. Caleb came in the shop, thought it was a leftover clip from the party, and had it uploaded within seconds."

Rachel's stomach locked down tight. "And you . . . all saw me . . . and how many others?"

Mike laughed. "The whole world."

"It's gone viral!" Andi exclaimed and held up her smartphone to show her the images. "You've already got 20,000 views on YouTube."

"You were an instant sensation," Kim added. "All of a sudden the phone started ringing with calls from women asking to be part of the cupcake club."

Rachel frowned. "Why?"

"Because you were honest and connected with women

on a personal level," Andi told her and nodded to her phone. "Orders for cupcakes are pouring in. Three weddings, two birthday parties, and a booking for the Scandinavian Festival next month. There won't be any problem paying our rent on time."

"What I said *was* personal," Rachel said, trembling from the thought of being utterly exposed.

"Did you mean it?" Mike asked, turning her to face him. "What you said about never wanting to wear a mask again?"

"From now on, you will only see the real Rachel," she assured him. "I'm through with masks."

"So am I," Mike told her. "Right before you arrived, I met with the director of the new movie set to film in Astoria next month. He hired me to build a model of the *Peter Iredale.* I told him I knew a beautiful redhead who might like to play the part of one of the stowaways living an enchanted life at sea."

"I'm already living an enchanted life here in Astoria," she told him, "with *you.*"

Mike dropped down on one knee. "Rachel Marie Donovan, I knew how uncomfortable you were at the party and only backed off to give you space. You never 'lost' me. I love you and promise to always love you." He paused, then grinned. "Will you marry me?"

Rachel gasped. Out of the corner of her eye she saw Andi and Kim clutch each other's arms and heard them gasp, too.

"You'll love me even when I'm *not* 'stupendous'?" she asked, giving him a big teasing smile.

"Yes," he said, his eyes still locked on hers. "Will you love me even if I'm not always 'magnificent'?"

"Yes, Mike, I will!" Throwing her arms around his neck, she found she was laughing, crying, and deliriously happy all at the same time.

Mike stood up and lifted her off her feet. As he swung her around, a cheer rose into the air. Rachel looked toward the tracks and realized it came from the people on the trolley.

Mike also saw them watching and grinned again. Then he bent her backward and swept her up into a kiss so sweet, so tender, so *magnificent,* she lost all sense of her surroundings.

For at least two minutes. Until Mike pulled his mouth away to place a light kiss on the tip of her nose.

"I thought *I* was the impulsive one," Andi said and clapped as she jumped up and down. "After your wedding you can drive away in the Cupcake Mobile!"

"We can tie tin cans and tinsel to the bumper!" Kim added.

Rachel laughed, and Mike captured her lips again, this time holding nothing back, but drawing her in deep for a kiss that held the promise of never ending. She smiled inside, her heart soaring, as she dreamed of their new life together.

A life as sweet as a beautiful ship in full sail toward a horizon of blue sky and open sea.

Recipe for
DEEP CHOCOLATE CAKE

From Merrilee Shoop of Allyn, Washington

Combine all ingredients in a large bowl. Mix on slow to medium speed until well blended and smooth.

   3 cups flour
   2 cups sugar
   2 tsp. baking soda
   1 tsp. salt
   6 Tbsp. cocoa
   1 Tbsp. vinegar
   1 tsp. vanilla
   ¾ cup vegetable oil
   2 cups water

   Pour into a 13-by-9-inch pan (no need to grease and flour pan). Bake at 350° for 5 minutes and reduce heat to 300° for 45 minutes.

Frosting:
   5 tbsp. flour
   1 cup milk

   Cook in a pot over low heat and continue stirring to avoid lumps. When it forms a thick paste, set aside and let cool. In a medium bowl, mix:

1 cup sugar
1 cup butter
1 tsp. vanilla

Beat until fluffy, then add the flour and milk paste and beat until spreading consistency.

Keep reading for an excerpt from the first
book in THE CUPCAKE DIARIES series,

SWEET ON YOU

now available from Avon Impulse.
And catch a sneak peek at the third book in
THE CUPCAKE DIARIES series,

TASTE OF ROMANCE

available from Avon Impulse May 21, 2013.

An Excerpt from

THE CUPCAKE DIARIES: SWEET ON YOU

Forget love . . . I'd rather fall in chocolate!
—**Author unknown**

ANDI CAST A glance over the rowdy karaoke crowd to the man sitting at the front table with the clear plastic bakery box in his possession.

"What am I supposed to say?" she whispered, looking back at her sister, Kim, and their friend Rachel as the three of them huddled together. "Can I have your cupcake? He'll think I'm a lunatic."

"Say 'please,' and tell him about our tradition," Kim suggested.

"Offer him money." Rachel dug through her dilapidated Gucci knockoff purse and withdrew a ten-dollar bill. "And let him know we're celebrating your sister's birthday."

"You did promise me a cupcake for my birthday," Kim said with an impish grin. "Besides, the guy doesn't look like he plans to eat it. He hasn't even glanced at the cupcake since the old woman came in and delivered the box."

Andi tucked a loose strand of blond hair behind her ear and drew in a deep breath. She wasn't used to taking food from anyone. Usually she was on the other end—giving it away. Her fault. She didn't plan ahead.

Why couldn't any of the businesses here be open twenty-four hours like in Portland? Out of the two dozen eclectic cafes and restaurants along the Astoria waterfront promising to satisfy customers' palates, shouldn't at least one cater to late-night customers like herself? No, they all shut down at 10:30, some earlier, as if they knew she was coming. That's what she got for living in a small town. Anticipation but no cake.

However, she was determined not to let her younger sister down. She'd promised Kim a cupcake for her twenty-sixth birthday, and she'd try her best to procure one, even if it meant making a fool of herself.

Andi shot her ever-popular friend Rachel a wry look. "You know you're better at this than I am."

Rachel grinned. "You're going to have to start interacting with the opposite sex again sometime."

Maybe. But not on the personal level, Rachel's tone suggested. Andi's divorce the previous year had left behind a bitter aftertaste no amount of sweet talk could dissolve.

Pushing back her chair, she stood up. "Tonight, all I want is the cupcake."

ANDI HAD TAKEN only a few steps when the man with the bakery box turned his head and smiled.

He probably thought she was coming over, hoping to find a date. Why shouldn't he? The Captain's Port was filled with people looking for a connection, if not for a lifetime, then at least for the time they shared within the friendly confines of the restaurant's casual, communal atmosphere.

She hesitated midstep before continuing forward. Heat rushed into her cheeks. Dressed in jeans and a navy blue tie and sport jacket, he was even better looking than she'd first thought. Thirtyish. Light brown hair, fair skin, sparkling chocolate brown eyes, *oh my*. He could have his pick of any woman in the place. Any woman in Astoria, Oregon.

"Hi," he said.

Andi swallowed the nervous tension gathering at the back of her throat and managed a smile in return. "Hi. I'm sorry to bother you, but it's my sister's birthday, and I promised her a cupcake." She nodded toward the see-through box and waved the ten-dollar bill. "Is there any chance I can persuade you to sell the one you have here?"

His eyebrows shot up. "You want my cupcake?"

"I meant to bake a batch this afternoon," she gushed, her words tumbling over themselves, "but I ended up packing spring break lunches for the needy kids in the school district. Have you heard of the Kids' Coalition backpack program?"

He nodded. "Yes, I think the *Astoria Sun* featured the free lunch backpack program on the community page a few weeks ago."

"I'm a volunteer," she explained. "And after I finished, I tried to buy a cupcake but didn't get to the store in time. I've never let my sister down before, and I feel awful."

The new addition to her list of top ten dream-worthy males leaned back in his chair and pressed his lips together, as if considering her request, then shook his head. "I'd love to help you, but—"

"*Please.*" Andi gasped, appalled she'd stooped to begging. She straightened her shoulders and lifted her chin. "I understand if you can't, it's just that my sister, Kim, my friend Rachel, and I have a tradition."

"What kind of tradition?"

Andi pointed to their table, and Kim and Rachel smiled and waved. "Our birthdays are spaced four months apart, so we split a celebration cupcake three ways and set new goals for ourselves from one person's birthday to the next. It's easier than trying to set goals for an entire year."

"I don't suppose you could set your goals without the cupcake?" he asked, his eyes sparkling with amusement.

Andi smiled. "It wouldn't be the same."

"If the cupcake were mine to give, it would be yours. But this particular cupcake was delivered for a research project I have at work."

"Wish I had your job." Andi dropped into the chair he pulled out for her and placed her hands flat on the table.

"What if I told you it's been a really tough day, tough week, tough year?"

He pushed his empty coffee cup aside, and the corners of his mouth twitched upward. "I'd say I could argue the same."

"But did you spend the last three hours running all over town looking for a cupcake?" she challenged, playfully mimicking Rachel's flirtatious, sing-song tone. "The Pig 'n Pancake was closed, along with the supermarket, and the café down the street said they don't even sell them anymore. And then . . . I met you."

He covered her left hand with his own, and although the unexpected contact made her jump, she ignored the impulse to pull her fingers away. His gesture seemed more an act of compassion than anything else, and, frankly, she liked the feel of his firm yet gentle touch.

"What if I told you," he said, leaning forward, "that I've traveled five hundred and seventy miles and waited sixty-three days to taste this one cupcake?"

Andi leaned toward him as well. "I'd say that's ridiculous. There's no cupcake in Astoria worth all that trouble."

"What if this particular cupcake isn't from Astoria?"

"No?" She took another look at the box but didn't see a label. "Where's it from?"

"Hollande's French Pastry Parlor outside of Portland."

"What if I told you I would send you a dozen Hollande's cupcakes tomorrow?"

"What if I told *you*," he said, stopping to release a deep, throaty chuckle, "this is the last morsel of food I have to eat before I starve to death today?"

Andi laughed. "I'd say that's a good way to go. Or I could invite you to my place and cook you dinner."

Her heart stopped, stunned by her own words, then rebooted a moment later when their gazes locked, and he smiled at her.

"You can have the cupcake on one condition."

"Which is?"

Giving her a wink, he slid the bakery box toward her. Then he leaned his head in close and whispered in her ear.

An Excerpt from

THE CUPCAKE DIARIES: TASTE OF ROMANCE

All I really need is love, but a little chocolate now
and then doesn't hurt!

—Charles Schulz

Focus, KIM REPRIMANDED herself. *Keep to the task at hand and stop eavesdropping on other people's conversations.*

But she didn't need to hear the crack of the teenage boy's heart to feel his pain. Or to remember the last time she'd heard the wretched words "I'm leaving" spoken to her.

She tried to ignore the couple as she picked up the pastry bag filled with pink icing and continued to decorate the tops of the strawberry preserve cupcakes. However, the discussion between the high school boy and what she assumed to be his girlfriend kept her attentive.

"When will I see you again?" he asked.

Kim glanced toward them, leaned closer, and held her breath.

"I don't know," the girl replied.

The soft lilt in her accent thrust the familiarity of the conversation even deeper into Kim's soul.

"I'll be going to the university for two years," the girl continued. "Maybe we meet again after."

Not likely. Kim shook her head, and her stomach tightened. From past experience, she knew once the school year was over in June, most foreign students went home, never to return.

And left many broken hearts in their wake.

"Two years is a long time," the boy said.

Forever was even longer. Kim drew in a deep breath as the unmistakable catch in the poor boy's voice replayed again and again in her mind. And her heart.

How long were they going to stand there and torment her and remind her of her parting four years earlier with Gavin, the Irish student she'd dated through college? Dropping the bag of icing on the Creative Cupcakes counter, she moved toward them.

"Can I help you?" Kim asked, pulling on a new pair of food handler's gloves.

"I'll have the white chocolate macadamia," the girl said, pointing to the cupcake she wanted in the glass display case.

The boy dug his hands into his pockets, counted the

meager change he'd managed to withdraw, and turned five shades of red.

"None for me." His Adam's apple bobbed as he swallowed. "How much for hers?"

"You have to have one, too," the girl protested. "It's your birthday."

Kim took one look at his lost-for-words expression and said, "If today is your birthday, the cupcakes are free." She added, "For both you and your guest."

The teenage boy's face brightened. "Really?"

Kim nodded and removed the cupcakes the two lovebirds wanted from the display case. She even put a birthday candle on one of them, a heart on the other. Maybe the girl would come back for him. Or he would fly to Ireland for her. *Maybe*.

Her eyes stung, and she squeezed them shut for a brief second. When she opened them again, she set her jaw. Enough was enough. Now that they had their cupcakes, she could escape back into her work and forget about romance and relationships and every regrettable moment she'd ever wasted on love.

She didn't need it. Not like her older sister, Andi, who had recently lost her heart to Jake Hartman, their Creative Cupcakes financer and news writer for the *Astoria Sun*. Or like her other co-owner friend, Rachel, who had just gotten engaged to Mike Palmer, a miniature model maker for movies who also doubled as the driver of their Cupcake Mobile.

All she needed was to dive deep into her desire to put paint on canvas. She glanced at the walls of the cupcake shop, adorned with her scenic oil, acrylic, and watercolor paintings. Maybe if she worked hard enough, she'd have the money to open her own art gallery, and she wouldn't need to decorate cupcakes anymore.

But for now, she needed to serve the next customer. *Where was Rachel?*

"Hi, Kim." Officer Ian Lockwell, one of their biggest cupcake supporters, sat on one of the stools lining the marble cupcake counter. "I'm wondering if you have the back party room available on June twenty-seventh?"

Kim reached under the counter and pulled out the three-ring binder she, Andi, and Rachel had dubbed the "Cupcake Diary" to keep track of all things cupcake related. Looking at the calendar, she said, "Yes, the date is open. What's the occasion?"

"My wife and I have been married almost fifteen years," the big square-jawed cop told her. "We're planning on renewing our vows on our anniversary and need a place to celebrate with friends and family."

"No better place to celebrate love than Creative Cupcakes," Kim assured him, glancing around at all the couples in the shop. "I'll put you on the schedule."

Next, the door opened, and a stream of romance writers filed in for their weekly meeting. Kim pressed her lips together. The group intimidated her with their watchful eyes and poised pens. They scribbled in their notebooks whenever she walked by as if writing down her every move, and she didn't want to give them any useful fodder. She hoped Rachel could take their orders, if she could find her.

"Rachel?"

No answer, but the phone rang—a welcome distraction. She picked up and said, "Creative Cupcakes, this is Kim."

"What are you doing there? I thought you were going to take time off."

Kim pushed into the privacy of the kitchen, glad it was her sister, Andi, and not another customer despite the impending lecture tone. "I still have several dozen cupcakes to decorate."

"Isn't Rachel there with you?"

The door of the walk-in pantry burst open, and Rachel and Mike emerged, wrapped in each other's arms, laughing and grinning.

Kim rolled her eyes. "Yes, Rachel's here."

Rachel extracted herself from Mike's embrace and mouthed the word "Sorry."

But Kim knew she wasn't. Rachel had been in her own red-headed, happy bubble ever since macho, dark-haired Mike the Magnificent had proposed two weeks earlier.

"I'll be in for my shift as soon as I get Mia off to afternoon kindergarten," Andi continued, "and the shop's way ahead in sales. There's no reason you can't take a break. Ever since you broke up with Gavin, you've become a workaholic."

Kim sucked in her breath at the mention of his name. Only Andi dared to ever bring him up.

"Gavin has nothing to do with my work."

"You never date."

"I'm concentrating on my career."

"It's been years since you've been out with anyone. You need to slow down, take time to smell the roses."

"Smell the roses?" Kim gasped. "Are you *serious*?"

"Go on an adventure," Andi amended.

"Working is an adventure."

"You used to dream of a different kind of adventure," Andi said, lowering her voice. "The kind that requires a passport."

Kim wished she'd never picked up the phone. Just because her sister had her life put back together didn't mean she had the right to tell her how to live.

"Painting cupcakes and canvas is the only adventure I need right now. I promised Dad I'd have the money to pay him for my new art easel by the end of the week."

"Dad doesn't care about the money, but he does care about you. He asked me to call."

"He did?" Kim stopped in front of the sink and rubbed her temples with her fingertips. Her sister was known to overreact, but their father? He didn't voice concern unless it was legitimate.

With the phone to her ear, she returned to the front counter of the couple-filled cupcake shop, her heart screaming louder and louder with each consecutive beat.

They were *everywhere*. By the window, at the tables, next to the display case. Couples, couples, couples. Everyone had a partner, had someone.

Almost everyone.

Instead of Goonies Day, the celebration of the 1985 release date of *The Goonies* movie, which was filmed in Astoria, she would have thought the calendar had been flipped back to Valentine's Day at Creative Cupcakes. And in her opinion, one Valentine's Day a year was more than enough.

She reached a hand into the pocket of her pink apron and clenched the golden wings she had received on her first airplane flight as a child. The pin never left her side, and like the flying squirrel tattooed on her shoulder, it reminded her of her dream to fly, if not to another land, then at least to the farthest reaches of her imagination.

Where her heart would be free.

Okay, maybe she *did* spend too much time at the cupcake shop. "Tell Dad not to worry," Kim said into the phone. "Tell him . . . I'm taking the afternoon off."

"Promise?" Andi persisted.

Oh, yeah. Tearing off her apron, she turned around and threw it over Rachel's and Mike's heads. "I'm heading out the door now."

FIVE MINUTES LATER, Kim stood outside the cupcake shop on Marine Drive, wondering which direction to head. The tattoo parlor was on her left, a boutique to her right, and the waterfront walk beneath the giant arching framework of the Astoria–Megler Bridge stretched straight in front.

Turning her back on it all, she decided to take a new path and soon discovered an open wrought iron gate along Bond Road. The side entrance, she assumed, to Astoria's new community park. Hadn't her sister told her to "smell the roses"?

Kim walked through the gate toward a large circle of white rosebushes and began to count off each flower as she leaned in to fill her lungs with their strong, fragrant scent. "One, two, three . . ."

After smelling seventeen, she moved toward the yellows. "Eighteen, nineteen, twenty . . ."

Past the gazebo she found red roses, orange roses, and a vast variety of purples and pinks. "Forty-six, forty-seven, forty-eight . . ."

Her artist's eye took in the palette of color, and imagining the scene on canvas, she wished she'd brought along her paints and brushes. "Sixty-two, sixty-three, sixty-four . . ."

Andi had been right. The sweet, perfumed scent of the roses did seem to ease her tension and help block out all thoughts of romance. Even if the rose was a notorious symbol of *love*. And the flower that garnished the most sales over *romantic* holidays. With petals used for flower girl baskets at *weddings*.

Who needed romance anyway? Not her.

She bent to smell the next group of flowers and noticed a tall, blond man with work gloves carrying a potted rosebush past the ivy trellis. As his gaze caught hers, he appeared to pause. Then he smiled.

Kim smiled back and moved toward the next rose.

"Can I help you?" the gardener asked, walking over.

Oh, *no*. He had a foreign accent, Scandinavian, like some of the locals whose ancestors first inhabited the area. And she had an acute weakness for foreign accents.

"I think I need to do this myself," Kim replied. "My goal is to smell a hundred roses."

"Why a hundred?"

"That's the number of things on my to-do list. I thought stopping to smell one rose per task might balance out my life."

"Interesting concept." The attractive gardener appeared to suppress a grin. "How many more do you have to go?"

"I'm at sixty-seven."

"I didn't mean to interrupt." He set the rosebush down, took off a glove, and extended his hand. "I'm Nathaniel Sjölander."

"Kimberly Burke," she said, accepting the handshake. His hand, much larger than her own, surrounded her with warmth.

"I have to load a couple dozen roses into my truck for the Portland Rose Festival tomorrow, but by all means—keep sniffing."

Kim pulled rose number sixty-eight toward her, a yellow flower as buttery and delicately layered as a ... freshly baked croissant. Hunger sprang to life inside her empty stomach, and she realized she'd been so busy working, she'd forgotten to eat lunch.

She watched Nathaniel Sjölander move between the potted plants. Was he single? Would someone like him be interested in her? Maybe ask her to dinner? And why *hadn't* she dated anyone in the last few years? She could argue that good-looking single men were hard to come by, but the truth was, she just hadn't taken the initiative to find one.

Nathaniel made several trips back and forth between

the greenhouse and the gate, his gaze sliding toward her again and again. *Oh, yes!* He was definitely interested. Her pulse quickened as he approached her a second time.

"I think you missed a few." Nathaniel pulled a cut bouquet of red roses from behind his back and presented them to her.

"Thank you." She hugged the flowers against her chest and lifted her gaze from the Sjölander's Garden Nursery business logo embroidered on his tan work shirt to his warm, kind . . . *blue* eyes.

Oh, man, why did they have to be *blue*? Blue was her favorite color. She could get lost in blue. Especially *his* blue, a blend of sparkling azure with a hint of sea green. They reminded her of the ripples in the water where the Columbia River met the Pacific Ocean just outside Astoria.

"Sjölander. Is that Finnish?" she asked.

"Swedish. Most of my family resides in Sweden, with the exception of my brother and a few cousins."

His name was incredibly familiar. Where had she come across the name Sjölander before? The Cupcake Diary!

"I'm co-owner of Creative Cupcakes," Kim informed him. "Didn't you book us for an upcoming event?"

"Must be for the wedding."

Wedding? She held her breath. "*Yours?*"

He flashed her a smile. "No. My brother's."

"Of course." She breathed easy once again.

"They've decided to have the ceremony in the new community park."

Kim looked around, confused. "Isn't *this* the new community park?"

Nathaniel's eyes sparkled. "The park is two blocks down the street and much larger than my backyard."

"Your *backyard*?"

Kim's mouth popped open in an embarrassed "*O.*" Heat seared her cheeks. No wonder he'd been watching her. He was probably wondering what crazy chick was wandering around his property!

And as for the flowers? She doubted he meant them to symbolize anything romantic. Why would he? She was an idiot! The guy was probably just trying to be nice. Or maybe he thought giving her flowers would encourage her to leave. Worse—she would have to face him again in a few weeks at his brother's wedding.

With an inward groan she squeezed her eyes shut, wishing she could start the day over. Or maybe the whole last decade. Then without further ado she set her jaw and looked up.

"Thanks for the roses," she mumbled. And before she could embarrass herself further, she hurried out the gate and back to the cupcake shop—where she belonged.

Acknowledgments

I'D LIKE TO thank my editor at Avon Books, Lucia Macro, for giving me the opportunity to write this book series. It's been a dream come true.

And I'd like to thank my critique partners Jennifer Conner, D.V. Berkom, Chris Karlsen, and Wanda DeGolier for their inspiration and support.

About the Author

Darlene Panzera writes sweet, fun-loving romance and is a member of the Romance Writers of America's Greater Seattle and Peninsula chapters. Her career launched when her novella *The Bet* was picked by Avon Books and *New York Times* bestselling author Debbie Macomber to be published within Debbie's own novel, *Family Affair*. Darlene says, "I love writing stories that help inspire people to laugh, value relationships, and pursue their dreams."

Born and raised in New Jersey, Darlene is now a resident of the Pacific Northwest, where she lives with her husband and three children. When not writing she enjoys spending time with her family and her two horses and loves camping, hiking, photography, and lazy days at the lake.

Join her on Facebook or at www.darlenepanzera.com.

Visit www.AuthorTracker.com for exclusive information on your favorite HarperCollins authors.

Give in to your impulses . . .
Read on for a sneak peek at five brand-new
e-book original tales of romance
from Avon Books.
Available now wherever e-books are sold.

STEALING HOME
A DIAMONDS AND DUGOUTS NOVEL
By Jennifer Seasons

LUCKY LIKE US
BOOK TWO: THE HUNTED SERIES
By Jennifer Ryan

STUCK ON YOU
By Cheryl Harper

THE RIGHT BRIDE
BOOK THREE: THE HUNTED SERIES
By Jennifer Ryan

LACHLAN'S BRIDE
HIGHLAND LAIRDS TRILOGY
By Kathleen Harrington

An Excerpt from

STEALING HOME
A Diamonds and Dugouts Novel

by Jennifer Seasons

When Lorelei Littleton steals Mark Cutter's good
luck charm, all the pro ball player can think is
how good she looked . . . and how bad she'll pay.
Thrust into a contest of wills, they'll both discover
that while revenge may be a dish best served cold,
when it comes to passion, the hotter the better!

Raising his glass, Mark smiled and said, "To the rodeo. May you ride your bronc well."

Color tinged Lorelei's cheeks as they tapped their glasses. But her eyes remained on his while he took a long pull of smooth aged whiskey.

Then she spoke, her voice low. "I'll make your head spin, cowboy. That I promise."

That surprised a laugh out of him, even as heat began to pool heavy in his groin. "I'll drink to that." And he did. He lifted the glass and drained it, suddenly anxious to get on to the next stage. A drop of liquid shimmered on her full bottom lip, and it beckoned him. Reaching an arm out, Mark pulled her close and leaned down. With his eyes on hers, he slowly licked the drop off, his tongue teasing her pouty mouth until she released a soft moan.

Arousal coursed through him at the provocative sound.

Pulling her more fully against him, Mark deepened the kiss. Her lush little body fit perfectly against him, and her lips melted under the heat of his. He slid a hand up her back and fisted the dark, thick mass of her long hair. He loved the feel of the cool, silky strands against his skin.

He wanted more.

Tugging gently, Mark encouraged her mouth to open for him. When it did, his tongue slid inside and tasted, explored the exotic flavor of her. Hunger spiked inside him, and he took the kiss deeper. Hotter. She whimpered into his mouth and dug her fingers into his hair, pulled. Her body began pushing against his, restless and searching.

Mark felt like he'd been tossed into an incinerator when he pushed a thigh between her long, shapely legs and discovered the heat there. He groaned and rubbed his thigh against her, feeling her tremble in response.

Suddenly she broke the kiss and pushed out of his arms. Her breathing was ragged, her lips red and swollen from his kiss. Confusion and desire mixed like a heady concoction in his blood, but before he could say anything, she turned and began walking toward the hallway to his bedroom.

At the entrance she stopped and beckoned to him. "Come and get me, catcher."

So she wanted to play, did she? Hell yeah. Games were his life.

Mark toed off his shoes as he yanked his sweater over his head and tossed it on the floor. He began working the button of his fly and strode after her. He was a little unsteady on his feet, but he didn't care. He just wanted to catch her. When he entered his room, he found her by the bed. She'd turned on the bedside lamp, and the light illuminated every gorgeous inch of her curvaceous body.

He started toward her, but she shook her head. "I want you to sit on the bed."

Mark walked to her anyway and gave her a deep, hungry kiss before he sat on the edge of the bed. He wondered what she had in store for him and felt his gut tighten in anticipation. "Are you going to put on a show for me?" *God, it'd be so hot if she did.*

All she said was "mmm hmm." Then she turned her back to him. Mark let his eyes wander over her body and decided her tight, round ass in denim was just about the sexiest thing he'd ever seen.

When his gaze rose back up, he found her smiling over her shoulder at him. "Are you ready for the ride of your life, cowboy?"

Hell yes he was. "Bring it, baby. Show me what you've got."

Her smile grew sultry with unspoken promise as she reached for the hem of her t-shirt. She pulled it up leisurely while she kept eye contact with him. All he could hear was the soft sound of fabric rustling, but it fueled him—this seductively slow striptease she was giving him.

He wanted to see more of her. "Turn around."

As she turned, she continued to pull her shirt up until she was facing him with the yellow cotton dangling loosely from her fingertips. A black, lacy bra barely covered the most voluptuous, gorgeous pair of breasts he'd ever laid eyes on. He couldn't stop staring.

"Do you like what you see?"

Good God, yes. The woman was a goddess. He nodded, a

little harder than he meant to because he almost fell forward. He was starting to tell her how sexy she was when suddenly a full-blown wave of dizziness hit him. He shook his head to clear it. *What the hell?*

"Is everything all right, Mark?"

The room started spinning, and he tried to stand but couldn't. It felt like the world had been tipped sideways and his body was sliding onto the floor. He tried to stand again but fell backward onto the bed instead. He stared up at her as he tried to right himself and couldn't.

Fonda stood there like a siren, dark hair tousled around her head, breasts barely contained—guilt plastered across her stunning face.

Before he fell unconscious on the bed, he knew. Knew it with gut certainty. He tried to tell her, but his mouth wouldn't move. *Son of a bitch.*

Fonda Peters had drugged him.

An Excerpt from

LUCKY LIKE US

Book Two: The Hunted Series

by Jennifer Ryan

The second installment in The Hunted Series
by Jennifer Ryan . . .

1

A wisp of smoke rose from the barrel of his gun. The smell of gunpowder filled the air. Face raised to the night sky, eyes closed, he sucked in a deep breath and let it out slowly, enjoying the moment. Adrenaline coursed through his veins with a thrill that left a tingle in his skin. His heart pounded, and he felt more alive than he remembered feeling ever in his normal life.

Slowly, he lowered his head to the bloody body lying sprawled on the dirty pavement at his feet. The Silver Fox strikes again. The smile spread across his face. He loved the nickname the press had given him after the police spoke of the elusive killer who'd caused at least eight deaths—who knew how many more? He did. He remembered every one of them in minute detail.

He kicked the dead guy in the ribs. Sonofabitch almost ruined everything, but you didn't get to be in his position by leaving the details in a partnership to chance. They'd had a deal, but the idiot had gotten greedy, making him sloppy. He'd set up a meeting for tonight with a new hit but hadn't done the proper background investigation. His death was a direct result of his stupidity.

"You set me up with a cop!" he yelled at the corpse.

He dragged the body by the foot into the steel container, heedless of the man's face scraping across the rough road. He dropped the guy's leg. The loud thud echoed through the cavernous interior. He locked the door and walked through the deserted shipyard, indifferent.

Maybe he'd let his fury get the best of him, but anything, or anyone, who threatened to expose him or end his most enjoyable hobby needed to be eliminated. He had too much to lose, and he never lost.

Only one more loose end to tie up.

2

San Francisco
Thursday, 9:11 p.m.

Little devils stomped up Sam's spine, telling him trouble was on the way. He rolled his shoulders to erase the eerie feeling, but it didn't work, never did. He sensed something was wrong, and he'd learned to trust his instincts. They'd saved his hide more than once.

Sam and his FBI partner, Special Agent Tyler Reed, sat

in their dark car watching the entrance to Ray's Rock House. Every time someone opened the front door, the blare of music poured out into the otherwise quiet street. Sam's contact hadn't arrived yet, but that was what happened when you relied on the less reputable members of society.

"I've got a weird vibe about this," Sam said, breaking the silence. "Watch the front and alley entrances after I go in."

Tyler never took his eyes off the door and the people coming and going. "I've got your back, but I still think we need more agents on this. What's with you lately? Ever since your brother got married and had a family, you've been on edge, taking one dangerous case after another."

Sam remembered the way his brother looked at his wife and the jealousy that had bubbled up in his gut, taking him by surprise. Jenna was everything to Jack, and since they were identical twins, it was easy for Sam to put himself in Jack's shoes. All he had to do was look at Jack, Jenna, and their two boys to see what it would be like if he found someone to share his life.

Sam had helped Jenna get rid of her abusive ex-husband, who'd kidnapped her a couple years before. Until Jack had come into her life, she'd been alone, hiding from her ex— simply existing, she'd said. Very much like him.

An Excerpt from

STUCK ON YOU

by Cheryl Harper

Love's in the limelight when big-shot producer
KT Masters accidentally picks a fight with
Laura Charles, a single mother working as
a showgirl waitress in a hotel bar. When he
offers her the fling of a lifetime, Laura's willing
to play along . . . just so long as her heart
stays out of it. If she can help it, that is!

Laura said, "Excuse me, Mr. Masters." When he held up an impatient hand, she narrowed her eyes and turned back to the two women. "Maybe you can tell him the drinks are here? I've got other customers to take care of."

The pink-haired woman held out a hand. "Sure thing. I'm Mandy, the makeup artist. This is Shane. She'll do hair. We'll both help with costumes and props as needed."

As Laura shook their hands, she privately thought that might be the best arrangement. Shane's hair was perfect, not one strand out of place. Mandy's pink shag sort of made it look like she'd been caught in a windstorm. In a convertible. But her makeup and clothes were very cute.

KT said, "Hold on just a sec, Bob. Let me go ahead and tweet this. Gotta keep the fans interested, you know."

Laura glanced over her bare shoulder to see KT bound down the stairs, pause, snap a picture, and then type something on his phone before shouting about taking down the electronic display in the corner. Lucky would not be happy about that. As KT waved his arms dramatically and the director nodded, Laura smiled at the two girls. "Guess I'm dismissed."

They laughed, and Laura turned to skirt their table as she reached for the drink tray. Being unable to move, like her feathers had attached themselves to the floor, was her first clue that something had gone horribly wrong. And when KT Masters bumped into her, sending the tray skidding into the sodas she'd just delivered, she knew exactly who was responsible. She tried to whirl around to give him a piece of her mind but spun in place and then heard a loud rip just before she bumped into the table and sent two glasses crashing to the floor. She might have followed them, but KT wrapped a hand around her arm to steady her. His warm skin was a brand against her chilly flesh.

The only sound in Viva Las Vegas was the tinny *plink* of electricity through one million bright white bulbs. Every eye was focused on the drama taking place at the foot of the stage. Before she could really get a firm grip on the embarrassment, irritation, shock, and downright anger boiling over, Laura shouted, "You ripped off my feather!"

Even the light bulbs seemed to hold their breath at that point.

KT's hand slid down her arm, raising goose bumps as it went, before he slammed both hands on his hips, and Laura shivered. The heat from that one hand made her wonder what it would be like to be pressed up against him. Instead of the flannel robe, she should put a KT Masters on her birthday list. She wouldn't have to worry about being cold ever again.

"Yeah, I did you a favor. This costume has real potential"— he motioned with one hand as he looked her over from collarbone to knee—"but the feathers get in the way, so . . . you're welcome!" The frown looked all wrong on his face, like he didn't have a lot of experience with anger or irritation, but the look in his eyes was as warm as his hand had been. When he rubbed his palms together, she thought maybe she wasn't the only one to be surprised by the heat.

They both looked down at the bedraggled pink feather, now swimming in ice cubes and spilled soda under his left shoe. No matter how much she hated the feathers or how valid his point about their ridiculousness was, she wasn't going to let him get away with this. He should apologize. Any decent person would.

"What are you going to do about it?" She plopped her hands on her own hips, thrust her chin out, and met his angry stare.

He straightened and flashed a grim smile before leaning down to scrape the feather up off the floor. He pinched the driest edge and held it out from his body. "Never heard 'the customer's always right,' have you?"

Laura snatched the feather away. "In what way are you a customer? I only see a too-important big shot who can't apologize."

His opened his mouth to say . . . something, then changed his mind and pointed a finger in her face instead. "Oh, really? I bet if I went to have a little talk with the manager or Miss

Willodean, they'd have a completely different take on what just happened here and who needs to apologize."

Laura narrowed her eyes and tilted her head. "Oh, really? I'll take that bet."

An Excerpt from

THE RIGHT BRIDE
Book Three: The Hunted Series
by Jennifer Ryan

The Hunted Series continues with this
third installment by Jennifer Ryan . . .

1

Shelly swiped the lip gloss wand across her lips, rolled them in and out to smooth out the color, and grinned at herself in the mirror, satisfied with the results. She pushed up her boobs, exposing just enough flesh to draw a man's attention, and keep it, but still not look too obvious.

"Perfect. He'll love it."

Ah, Cameron Shaw. Rich and powerful, sexy as hell, and kind in a way that made it easy to get what she wanted. Exactly the kind of husband she'd always dreamed about marrying.

Shelly had grown up in a nice middle class family. Ordinary. She desperately wanted to be anything but ordinary.

She'd grown up a plump youngster and a fat teenager. At fifteen, she'd resorted to binging and purging and starved herself thin. Skinny and beautiful—boys took notice. You can get a guy to do just about anything when you offer them hot sex. By the time she graduated high school, she'd transformed herself into the most popular girl in the place.

For Shelly, destined to live a glamorous life in a big house with servants and fancy cars and clothes, meeting Cameron in the restaurant had been a coup.

Executives and wealthy businessmen frequented the upscale restaurant. She'd gone fishing and landed her perfect catch. Now, she needed to hold on and reel in a marriage proposal.

2

Night fell outside Cameron's thirty-sixth-floor office window. Tired, he'd spent all day in meetings. For the president of Merrick International, long hours were the norm and sleepless nights were a frequent occurrence.

The sky darkened and beckoned the stars to come to life. If he were out on the water, and away from the glow of the city lights, he'd see them better, twinkling in all their brilliant glory.

He couldn't remember the last time he'd taken out the sailboat. He'd promised Emma he'd take her fishing. Every time he planned to go, something came up at work. More and more often, he put her off in favor of some deal or problem that couldn't wait. He needed to realign his priorities. His daughter deserved better.

He stared at the picture of his golden girl. Emma was five now and the image of her mother: long, wavy golden hair and deep blue eyes. She always looked at him with such love. He remembered Caroline looking at him the same way.

They'd been so happy when they discovered Caroline was pregnant. In the beginning, things had been so sweet. They'd lain awake at night talking about whether it would be a boy or a girl, what they'd name their child, and what they thought he or she would grow up to be.

He never thought he'd watch his daughter grow up without Caroline beside him.

The pregnancy took a turn in the sixth month when Caroline began having contractions. They gave her medication to stop them and put her on bed rest for the rest of the pregnancy.

One night he'd come home to find her pale and hurting. He rushed her to the hospital. Her blood pressure spiked, and the contractions started again. No amount of medication could stop them. Two hours later, when the contractions were really bad, the doctor came in to tell him Caroline's body was failing. Her liver and kidneys were shutting down.

Caroline was a wreck. He still heard her pleading for him to save the baby. She delivered their daughter six weeks early, then suffered a massive stroke and died without ever holding her child.

Cameron picked up the photograph and traced his daughter's face, the past haunting his thoughts. He'd spent three weeks in the Neonatal Intensive Care Unit, grieving for his wife and begging his daughter to live. Week four had been a turning point. He felt she'd spent three weeks mourning the loss of her mother and then decided to live for her father. She began eating on her own and gained weight quickly. Ten days later, Cameron finally took his daughter home. From then on, it had been the two of them.

Almost a year ago, he'd decided enough was enough. Emma needed a mother.

An Excerpt from

LACHLAN'S BRIDE
Highland Lairds Trilogy
by *Kathleen Harrington*

Lady Francine Walsingham can't believe
Lachlan MacRath, laird and pirate, is to be her
escort into Scotland. But trust him she must, for
Francine has no choice but to act as his lover to
keep her enemies at bay. When Lachlan first sees
Francine, the English beauty stirs his blood like
no woman has ever before. And now that they
must play the besotted couple so he can protect
her, Lachlan is determined to use all his seductive
prowess to properly woo her into his bed.

An Excerpt from

LACHLAN'S BRIDE

A Highland Laird's Fantasy

by Kathleen Harrington

May 1496
The Cheviot Hills
The Border Between England and Scotland

Stretched flat on the blood-soaked ground, Lachlan Mac-Rath gazed up at the cloudless morning sky and listened to the exhausted moans of the wounded.

The dead and the dying lay scattered across the lush spring grass. Overhead, the faint rays of dawn broke above the hill-tops as the buttercups and bluebells dipped and swayed in the soft breeze. The gruesome corpses were sprawled amidst the wildflowers, their vacant eyes staring upward to the heavens, the stumps of their severed arms and legs still oozing blood and gore. Dented helmets, broken swords, axes, and pikes gave mute testimony to the ferocity of the combatants. Here and there, a loyal destrier, trained to war, grazed calmly alongside its fallen master.

Following close upon daylight, the scavengers would come

creeping, ready to strip the bodies of anything worth a shilling: armor, dirks, boots, belts. If they were Scotsmen, he'd be in luck. If not, he'd soon be dead. There wasn't a blessed thing he could do but wait. He was pinned beneath his dead horse, and all efforts to free himself during the night had proven fruitless.

In the fierce battle of the evening before, the warriors on horseback had left behind all who'd fallen. Galloping across the open, rolling countryside, Scots and English had fought savagely, until it was too dark to tell friend from foe. There was no way of knowing the outcome of the battle, for victory had been determined miles away.

Hell, it was Lachlan's own damn fault. He'd come on the foray into England with King James for a lark. After delivering four new cannons to the castle at Roxburgh, along with the Flemish master gunners to fire them, he'd decided not to return to his ship immediately as planned. The uneventful crossing on the *Sea Hawk* from the Low Countries to Edinburgh, followed by the tedious journey to the fortress, with the big guns pulled by teams of oxen, had left him eager for a bit of adventure.

When he'd learned that the king was leading a small force into Northumberland to retrieve cattle raided by Sassenach outlaws, the temptation to join them had been too great to resist. There was nothing like a hand-to-hand skirmish with his ancient foe to get a man's blood pumping through his veins.

But Lord Dacre, Warden of the Marches, had surprised the Scots with a much larger, well-armed force of his own, and what should have been a carefree rout had turned into deadly combat.

A plea for help interrupted Lachlan's brooding thoughts.

Not far away, a wounded English soldier who'd cried out in pain during the night raised himself up on one elbow.

"Lychester! Over here, sir! It's Will Jeffries!"

Lachlan watched from beneath slit lids as another Sassenach came into view. Attired in the splendid armor of the nobility, the newcomer rode a large, caparisoned black horse. He'd clearly come looking for someone, for he held the reins of a smaller chestnut, its saddle empty and waiting.

"Here I am, Marquess," the young man named Jeffries called weakly. He lifted one hand in a trembling wave as the Marquess of Lychester drew near to his countryman. Dismounting, he approached the wounded soldier.

"Thank God," Jeffries said with a hoarse groan. "I've taken a sword blade in my thigh. The cut's been oozing steadily. I was afraid I wouldn't make it through the night."

Lychester didn't say a word. He came to stand behind the injured man, knelt down on one knee, and raised his fallen comrade to a seated position. Grabbing a hank of the man's yellow hair, the marquess jerked the fair head back and deftly slashed the exposed throat from ear to ear. Then he calmly wiped his blade on the youth's doublet, lifted him up in his arms, and threw the body facedown over the chestnut's back.

The English nobleman glanced around, checking, no doubt, to see if there'd been a witness to the coldblooded execution. Lachlan held his breath and remained motionless, his lids still lowered over his eyes. Apparently satisfied, the marquess mounted, grabbed the reins of the second horse, and rode away.

Lachlan slowly exhaled.

Sonofabitch.